A Passing Resemblance

LM Foster

This is a work of fiction. Names, characters, places and incidents are products of the author's imagination. Any resemblance to actual events, locales, organizations, or persons, either living or dead, is entirely coincidental.

Cover by
Ravenna Young
www.ravennayoung.blogspot.ca

9th Street Press
www.9thstreetpress.com

This book is dedicated to the men and women who work tirelessly to bring us the internet every day. Without them, our world would be a much less entertaining place.

ONE

When it comes to love, I am what you could call a *serial obsessionist*. Whenever I see a man that pleases me - all I have to do is *see* him, and I am just that easily, completely, in love. Ah, the water is fine, swimming neck deep in fullest infatuation! And then I must see him every day, must dreamily gaze upon the beautiful face at every possible opportunity; think nasty thoughts about the excellent body.

Then, after a while, the infatuation fades; the warm feelings ebb and subside. Or more usually, all of that just totally disappears in the skipped heartbeat when I behold the next one. Then it all starts again.

What's that you say? There's already a term for women who behave this way, and it's not *serial obsessionist*? There are actually *lots* of words for women who behave like this, and none of them are very nice. But all these names only apply if you are talking about women and their interactions with real, live, flesh and blood men.

But I'm not talking about *real* men. Oh, they're real enough, I guess, in that they exist. But I've never actually met any of them. I just fall in love with them in my head. This leads to pretty one-sided relationships, I'll give you that. But the habit never hurt me before, never brought me one bit of trouble. Or anyone else, either, at least not until recently. A perfectly harmless . . . *hobby*.

Why am I writing it down now? I've always said that anyone who writes things down: diaries, *confessions* - *wants* someone to read them. The protestations for privacy and that lock and key are just window dressing. Nothing is safe in black and white. If you don't want anyone to know about what happened, keep it to yourself, keep it locked up inside your head, don't tell anyone, and certainly don't *write it down.*

But truth be told, I like to talk to myself, like to hear myself talk, and if anyone ever gets a hold of this train wreck of a story, they would never believe it anyway. Besides, it's cold outside and I'm not sleepy. And not a creature is stirring, not even a mouse.

So what, precisely, is a serial obsessionist, anyway? That must be explained, as it's the driving force in my life, the thing that defines me. Yet it's something that I've learned to keep to myself. All harmless fun, a hidden part of my personality, really, something that I've only allowed to be glimpsed. Because a full frontal view might lead people to think I'm nuts.

A definition. Hmm. Call me a fan; a diminutive of the word *fanatic.* I'm too young to have been one of those hysterical Beatles fans, screaming and crying and orgasming all over the Ed Sullivan Show. But that's an accurate visual for the way I feel when thinking about this week's crush. But all on the inside, of course. Couldn't ever let it show in public like that. Have to hide the crazy. Have some dignity.

The objects have mostly been actors; there was one musician (twins, actually, but I favored one over the other). And not your really famous ones, either. No flies on the Brad Pitts and the George Clooneys of the world, mind you, but it seems that I always run across and obsess on the obscure actors, ones that never really got to be very famous. Or I seem to discover them right *before* they become famous.

And then there was that Canadian guy, but we will get to him in a minute. *Boy, will we get to him.*

It all started with a rerun of *Miami Vice.* It was the one where a nefarious gun dealer blows up Sonny's black car. But it wasn't Don Johnson who caught my attention, this time. Although Don was fine, I hadn't really obsessed on him. Liking an actor, just being a fan, is a totally different beast

2

from *obsession*. This will become abundantly clear in a moment.

Don's star, however dim, was about to be eclipsed by the actor playing the gun dealer, however. Allow me to paraphrase the scene for you.

The gun dealer is showing Crockett and Tubbs missile launchers out of a unit in a storage facility.

Crockett: *These are old. How do we know they work?*

Gun Dealer aims and blows up Crockett's Ferrari. Sonny looks over his sunglasses, open-mouthed.

Tubbs: *Sold!*

I had to wait until the end to find out the guy's name, just a supporting bad guy character. This is the very best part of the discovery process, that anticipation, when you say to yourself, "*Who was that?*" and then you find out his name, quick as a flash in those closing credits. Jeff Fahey. Oh, my God, those blue eyes! That low, gravelly voice. He was just so deliciously evil, so very bad!

Nowadays, once the newest object has been identified, one runs to the internet and starts hitting fan sites and downloading pictures. Later I'll sit in the dark in front of the computer, and study those same pictures, *and covet*, one by one, over and over again, like Silas Marner counting his money.

My discovery of Jeff was sometime in the mid 1990's and there wasn't much internet yet, in those days. There was Netscape, and you could buy a lot of movie posters online, but there weren't too many fan sites yet, not too many pictures available.

The only tools I had for real research were a copy of *The Videohound's Golden Movie Retriever* and a video store on every corner. So I began tracking down all the horrible, limited release (did I mention horrible?) movies he was ever in. Fortunately, I had two VCR's in those days and wasn't in the least bit afraid to use them, yo ho. (The first sin/crime mentioned in this confessional, but not hardly the last.)

He was in a movie called *Sketch Artist* with Sean Young, and *White Hunter, Black Heart* with Clint Eastwood, where Clint was playing a character based upon John Huston, of all people. He was in *Iron Maze* with Bridget Fonda. All of them were horrible.

He was in *Body Parts*, a decent horror film, which was followed by his break out role in *The Lawnmower Man* with Pierce Brosnan. He was a blonde in that one, and I watched it so many times that I knew the dialogue. Then I discovered *Silverado*, which had everybody in it (Kevin Kline, Costner, Jeff Goldblum and others). He played Tyree, one of the villains. It was a decent Western, if you go in for Westerns. I named a little orange cat that I found in an alley Tyree.

I bought movie posters. I thought impure thoughts. I looked for more movies. Try as I might, I never did find *The Serpent of Death*, wherein he supposedly played an archaeologist, of all things. But it's just as well. It was probably bad.

Somewhere in a box, to this very day, I still have *The Jeff Fahey Collection*, Volumes 1 through Whatever (sometimes you could get two movies on one VHS if you used Extra Long Play). Forgotten and dusty somewhere, complete with peeling, laboriously typed labels. I don't even have a VCR anymore, but I wouldn't give up that box of tapes for anything. Although Jeff, too, has been overshadowed, forgotten (he got old like the rest of us) - he does Quentin Tarantino movies these days - there is still a special place in my heart for him and those horrible videos, which I watched over and over and over. They never got any better, but he still looked great in every one of them. He was the first obsession. It lasted a good year, year and a half.

Then I spied (party like it's) 1999's *A Midsummer Night's Dream*, at *The Wherehouse* or *SuperDuper Video*, or one of them. I was very young at the time, but I had a membership to every video store in town.

I rented the movie. Everybody is in that one, too: Kevin Kline again, Stanley Tucci, Michele Pfieffer, David Strahairn,

Rupert Everett, Sam Rockwell, Callista. That French chick. But wait! Who was that playing Demetrius? *Who was that?* That perfect little bow mouth, those eyes. Credits, credits, credits . . . Roll, credits! Some guy I'd never heard of: *Christian Bale.*

I discovered Christian right before *American Psycho* came out, a lifetime before Batman and his flipping out on the stage hands. In fact, I went out of my way to actually read *American Psycho*, just because he was going to be in the movie version. And while I felt that Ellis very accurately captured the spirit of the times, I thought the whole thing was a little far-fetched. No one is crazy like that; no one is that crazy.

Anyway, after seeing *A Midsummer Night's Dream*, Jeff Fahey was forgotten. Pfft! Gone from my imagination, just like that. It was time to go to the internet and find out who this Christian Bale person was.

By the way, the four loveliest words in the English language are not, *I love you forever.* They are: *Device is internet ready*. Ah, the internet! How did we ever live, conquer continents, breed and thrive, build and invent, put a man on the moon, without the internet? How did we learn, how were we ever entertained?

The biggest thrill is the search. First, more pictures. More pictures, more pictures, more pictures of the lovely visage, already so dear, already becoming so very familiar. Eyes and smiles and different haircuts, little tics and mannerisms. By this time, the internet fan girl train was gathering its initial head of steam. It hasn't slowed down since. There were dozens of fan sites devoted to Christian, already. Dozens of girls who were just that extra shade crazier than me: I just looked at their sites. They actually took the time and effort to create them in the first place. And for that, I thank them, from the bottom of my heart.

When I was first obsessing on Christian Bale, the absolutely indispensable *Wikipedia*, the best thing to hit the internet since cats, hadn't yet been invented. Or, if it had, it hadn't yet appeared on my radar. I don't know why they're so against advertising; the man could make millions; billions. I understand that it all involves some kind of altruism that I don't comprehend, something about the internet being free and all that. But nothing in this world is free, except for air, and if you want it heated, cooled, or under pressure, you're going to have to pay for it. So, I would be willing to look at some advertisements instead of looking at the guy begging for money all the time. But I digress.

I've been told to take *Wikipedia* with a grain of salt, that it's made up by people, and people lie. But I'm not looking for great philosophical treatises on these fantasy objects from *Wikipedia* (leave that to fan sites). I just want a list of the movies they were in, and whether or not they're heterosexual, single or married. And that information is usually correct enough from *Wikipedia*.

Once you perused the list of his filmography, gleaned from whatever source (there's also IMDb), the coolest thing is if you find out that you've already seen him before in something else, and just hadn't realized it. I discovered that Christian had played the boy in another of my favorite Shakespeare movies, *Henry V*. Found out that he had in fact been quite the child actor.

Then the quest to find and view all the new hero's old movies begins. And the old movies, the before-he-was-famous movies? They're usually bad. Because if they weren't bad, then they would've been the movies that made him famous. Sometimes the movie isn't bad, sometimes he's just in a supporting role in it. But even then, it's still usually bad.

I had a friend that used to say that there were only two movies where you wanted the Nazis to win; one was *The Sound of Music*, and the other was *Swing Kids*. I didn't get a chance to see that one, but I'm sure it couldn't have been *that* bad. Well, maybe. I didn't get to see *Newsies*, either, mostly because I wasn't that interested in seeing him sing and dance.

I'll never forget all the Christian Bale movies I sat through, after that original blush of attraction from *A Midsummer Night's Dream*. There were no epics, unfortunately. He played quite the bastard in *Shaft*, even though the character was kind of a cartoon. He was just annoying in *Reign of Fire*; it was an annoying movie all around.

Equilibrium would've been the most original story ever told, if it hadn't been for *Fahrenheit 451* or Orwell's *1984* and or even that Apple Macintosh commercial from Super Bowl XVIII. *Equilibrium* was unapologetically derivative of all of these. And saying *derivative* is using a nice word. Someone less kind might say *copied* or even *stolen*. But the gunplay idea, that was original.

I was appalled by *The Machinist*; with that one, Christian slipped totally off the obsession table. He crawled back up there for a minute for *The Prestige*, which was an unusually, surprisingly original movie. I missed *3:10 to Yuma*, because I generally hate Westerns, and I figured also that I couldn't suspend disbelief long enough to believe an Englishman and an Australian as American Wild West gunslingers.

Seeing as I was a big Christian Bale fan, and I had a friend who was a big comic book fan, we were high on anticipation when the two of us went to see *The Dark Knight*, the night it opened. We walked into the theater with large hopes: I wanted to see Christian do some real acting; my friend wanted to see the vindication of the Batman franchise. Both of us were so disappointed that we had no choice but to go out and get drunk after it was over. Christian's star dimmed. I haven't gone out of my way to catch him in another thing.

The only trait that Jeff and Christian shared (they certainly don't look anything alike), is that both of them are actors' actors. If acting is to be thought of as a job, just like any other job, then it doesn't really matter what the part is, does it? Shakespeare is as good as a Hollywood blockbuster; *Miami Vice* or *Machete* is equal to that stupid serpent movie that I could never find. Work, apparently, is work, because these guys will appear in *anything*. No prima donna aspirations about waiting for the *right part* to come along. No high falutin' concepts about *art*. Work is work. I applaud them both for it.

TWO

And then dawned the day when I discovered a pair of musicians and their band. I learned so much from the experience of following this group of young men, that one might say it constituted the next step in the evolution of my serial obsessionist-ness. I caught their act strictly by accident, by chance, by serendipity. I didn't usually watch MTV: I'd grown far too old for it. I was in my mid-twenties. But on this particularly historic day, there I was, flipping through the channels. It had probably been three or four years since I'd thought, *Hey, I wonder what's on MTV?*

And there they were.

The first thing I noticed wasn't the song, but the singer. Perhaps that's just the way it is nowadays in our visual world. The video has become infinitely more important than the audio, at least for the initial ensnaring of the listener. And upon first seeing them, before ever completely listening to them, I was quite ensnared.

The singer had black hair and black eyes. He had a red mouth and pink cheeks that belied how very young he was. Very young. The next thing I noticed was that he and the lead guitar had to be brothers. Upon further viewings, it became abundantly clear that not only were they brothers, they were twins. *Twins, Basil!*

Oh, my God, but they were adorable! The lead wore his black hair short, slicked back; he favored wife-beaters, low slung, baggy pants and wallet chains. The guitar player wore his hair in liberty spikes, with a bright magenta splotch at the front. In the video he wore a sleeveless shirt and plaid, zippered pants. He had earrings and nose rings and lip rings, and lots of tattoos. They were so strange looking, so alien, so sexy, and so *young*.

I immediately hit the internet to find out who these boys were, where they were from, what their shtick was, and when they would be coming to town near me. I discovered that they were from the East Coast, did indeed call their sound punk (even though punk had died with Sid in New York City, as far as I was concerned), and they would be appearing in a neighboring town that very weekend, at a tiny fire trap called *Sparky's*, hardly more than a stage and a bar.

Although I was no groupie, no band aficionado, even I could tell that the size of the venue was a good indicator of how famous they were not.

So I got all dressed up in what I imagined to be the finest groupie attire and headed off to meet the boys in the band. The thought didn't enter my mind that it might not be possible for me to seduce the lead guitar. They were still nobodies after all, just starting out. It wasn't like they were The Rolling Stones. It wasn't like they were anyone who would ever in this lifetime even *open* for The Rolling Stones. I was attractive enough, a few years older than both them and their small group of fans, certainly no minor. I could see absolutely no reason why I wouldn't be able to borrow him for my pleasure. Isn't that what rock stars did? Even though I was new to this groupie thing, I figured I'd have no trouble at all.

The idea of an actual physical encounter with one of the desired ones thrilled me to the bone. Never before had I ever even considered actually meeting one of them. I imagined that actors, even ones that weren't that famous, were no doubt difficult to meet. So I'd never even attempted it. Now that would just be crazy, I thought, actually trying to *meet* one of them. What the fuck would I say to him?

But musicians put themselves right out there for consumption; the interaction between band and fan being the whole point. Movies were prerecorded, meant to be enjoyed in a dark room by yourself. Music, especially live music, was meant to be shared between the performer and the fan, was it not? That cosmic coming together that produced Woodstock and The Warped Tour and Coachella, and foggy, drug-damaged memories that lasted a lifetime?

9

I meant to make my own memories with this black-haired guitar player.

All was well in my mind with this plan until I actually saw him before the show, riding around on a little bicycle outside the club. That was how not famous they were; the whole band could stand around outside the venue, talking to their sparse followers, (and always did so, right up until sound check), without any danger of being mobbed.

As I say, all was going well with my plan, right up to that moment when I approached him to introduce myself. Now, I must say that I'm not a shy person. My mamma always said, "You never get anything in this world by being shy," and she would push me out in front if I was hanging back. Never before had I been afraid to approach anyone that I wished to meet, and so it was on this occasion. I marched right up to this not yet famous musician, and said, "Hi, would you sign my CD?"

He took it from me and scrawled his name across it with a Sharpie that he pulled from his pocket. Then he looked up at me with that adorable trademark squint and said, "Hi. I'm Benji."

And it was at this point, ladies and gentlemen, that I completely lost the power of speech. Utterly. Here I was, a grown, college-educated woman, and I suddenly could no longer form words. I was breathing the same air he was. He was standing right there, *right there in front of me*: I could reach out and touch him. All these revelations were too much for my brain to process. Not only did I forget my own name, I couldn't have said it, even if I could've recalled it. I opened and closed my mouth several times, like the oft mentioned fish drowning in the air. This continued for what seemed like an hour; all the while he was looking expectantly at me. Finally, I was able to remember my name and introduce myself.

I wanted to say, *So nice to meet you, what are you doing after the show?* Wink, wink, nudge, nudge, we are all adults here, *and allow me to be the first to offer you recreation for the evening.* But whatever dubious powers of seduction that

I flattered myself as possessing evaporated into the sultry twilight air. I just stood there, silent as the grave.

Instead, *he* said, "So nice to meet you," with nary an innuendo. "Thanks for coming out to see us."

My power of speech, my eloquence, returned long enough for me to gush, "I would not have missed it for the world!" like a school girl.

Before I could say more, other fans, who actually *were* school girls, crowded around him and I was pushed out of the way. Unhappy with my performance, my failure to schedule an assignation after the show, I looked around and soon spied the drummer, bass player, and second guitar standing nearby. I approached, requested an autograph from each.

I found that I had no trouble talking to *these* not famous personages. I was able to smile and make small talk and ask *them* what they might be doing after the show. They looked at each other, then back at me in embarrassment, and I realized that they were taking my question as a proposition, the way I would've intended it for Benji, had I been able to spit it out.

But these were nothing but semi-talented *boys*. They were neither Benji nor his twin brother, they of the black hair and smoldering brown eyes, the pink-tinged skin, like milk. I certainly wasn't propositioning them, either singly or as a group, and I hastened to dispel any impression that I was. I added, "I mean, what do rock stars usually do in a strange town after a show?"

The bass player humbly asserted that they weren't really rock stars, at least not yet. I was grateful that he seemed to understand now that I was just making conversation with him. He said, "We usually go right back to the hotel and go to sleep."

But he no doubt suspected again that I was angling for info of a more nefarious bent, as referenced either the front or his twin brother, when I said, "All of you?"

"Pretty much."

"Even Benji?"

"Especially Benji." The singer had appeared at my elbow. He nodded at his confreres and then looked at me again, and I could tell from his expression that he knew exactly what I was thinking, exactly what I'd come to the show looking for. And he was not having any.

For something to say, I asked him to sign my CD, babbled on about how much I loved their music. For some reason, even though they were twins, this one didn't rob me of my power of speech. He thanked me, but that expression remained, the one that said he knew exactly what or whom it was I loved, and that he was confident that his brother wouldn't be having any either.

The school girls discovered that the rest of the band was there, and once again I was pushed out of the way as they gathered around for autographs and small talk. I was dumbfounded. The question rang in my mind, and I couldn't answer it: how had I failed to make plans with this guy, who was actually just some poor boy from the East Coast, not famous, not twenty-five yet? To whence had my never-failed-me-before charm vanished?

But the show itself made me forget my consternation, underlined my aim to have this guitar player. Oh, my God, ladies (and gentlemen disposed that way), is there anything more sexy than a guitar player? The way he moves on stage, the way he holds, caresses, abuses his instrument; his head throw back in ecstasy one moment then up close whispering seductively into the mike the next? If all of this isn't the act simulated, I don't know what is. Like John Cougar said, *Forget all about that macho shit/And learn how to play guitar.* There is absolutely nothing sexier than a musician that one finds sexy. Cue those hysterically screaming Beatles fans.

Again the band gathered outside the venue after the show, standing around and talking to fans. I spoke to them again, got my picture taken with them. Bolstered by a few drinks (I was the only fan in evidence old enough to partake), I was even able to ask Benji if he had plans for the rest of the evening. He told me that they were all going back to the hotel and calling it a night. Something about getting up early for the trip to the next show in the next town. I wanted to tell him that I wouldn't take up more than a half an hour or so of his time at most, but it was obvious that he wasn't interested.

Denied.

I followed this band all over the West Coast for a year. When they saw me, night after night, standing outside, waiting in line, they never failed to say hi. After a couple of shows, after a couple cities, I felt compelled to explain to this guitar player that perhaps he'd misunderstood me. I hurried to explain that I hadn't actually been trying to make a pass at him at all. I was just a really big fan and wondered if maybe we could just grab a coffee or something after one of the shows, and just talk for a minute.

He graciously assured me that he had not just naturally assumed that I'd been trying to make a pass at him at all. But he somehow never found a moment to have that coffee with me, either. His brother never failed to look through me to my deepest desires, so I figured that I was found out, no matter what I said.

I befriended some of the young girls while we stood in the interminable lines. Or they befriended me actually, because I was there for conquest and not camaraderie, and I couldn't imagine why any other girl would want to be friendly when it was obvious that one of us would throw her companion eagerly under the bus if the guitar player that we both worshiped would casually choose her. But we commiserated and compared: the rumor was that they were just good boys; and that was why no one had ever heard of them picking any girls out of the crowd. As an adult, this was something that I simply refused to believe.

In San Francisco, the band was standing just a little off to one side before the show. I waved and they waved, but I couldn't go over and speak to them, because I would lose my place in line. There was that velvet rope that would always separate us.

I noticed a young woman come up, give the bass player a hug, then speak animatedly to the whole band for several minutes. The last thing the bass player said was, "We'll see you after the show!" Then they went in the venue through a side door.

The girl walked toward the line, and I said, "Hey, can I ask you something?"

She paused and smiled at me. "Sure."

"Do you *know* them?"

Her smile widened. She understood, implicitly, what I meant. "As a matter of fact I do. We went to high school together. I heard that they were here in town, so I thought I would come out and show 'em some support."

"Can you tell me something? Do they ever, you know, *choose any girls* - do they all have girlfriends or something?" I felt ridiculous, asking such ridiculous high school questions, but I had to know why I wasn't getting any action. Why not me? What was the problem? There was no obvious reason for him not to choose me.

"No, they're all single."

"Do they ever, you know, pick any girls out of the crowd?"

She narrowed her eyes at me, but her smile never dimmed. "No, not really. I think that it might be in their contract that they can't." She gestured at the girls in line. "They're all underage. The guys, they could get in a lot of trouble."

"I'm not underage," I said ruefully.

Still she smiled, and now it was tinged with a little pity. "There's a difference between girlfriends and fans. I've known them for years. In fact, I had a little thing with the bass player back in high school."

"Can I buy you a drink, once we get inside?" Now she looked suspicious. "No, I wouldn't try to get at them through one of their friends. It's just rare to meet anyone old enough to drink at any of their shows."

She nodded and we sat at the bar for the show, the only one where I wouldn't be up front on the rail. She explained this concept for me in its entirety, this monumental difference between friends and fans. Friends were someone you knew, someone who knew you, someone who knew what kind of beer you drank. Friends knew your cell phone number. Friends didn't lose their hillbilly minds when you walked out on stage.

Fans were the ones for whom you had to keep up appearances (or appear to be bad boys for). They were the ones to whom you had to shill the CD's and t-shirts. Fans were the ones who knew what beer the *record company* said you drank. Fans were a paycheck.

"You're the one that's been to every show for the last year, huh?" she asked.

Facepalm. *"They talk about me?"*

She smiled kindly, nodded. "You're what they call a *rabid* fan."

And it was then that I realized that I would never jump from fan to friend, no matter what I did. It didn't matter how attractive I was, how not underage I was. I was that nutball chick that had followed them like the Roman Army up and down the West Coast, and no matter what happened, they would always be suspicious of me.

Friends were people that knew you. Fans were people that worshiped you, and even though it's all a part of the game, everybody is a little weirded out by fans like me. *Rabid fans.* The performers, their manager, the guy that drives the tour bus. Everybody is weirded out by it.

So the eternal question of *Why not me?* was finally answered. Friends were people that you met through other friends, who treated you just like other people, who were not impressed. Fans were just part of doing business, and never, *ever,* would the twain meet.

It was not fair, but it was the truth. It was a lesson that I wouldn't soon forget, a mistake that I would not make again.

THREE

I ceased to follow the band when I met and started dating dear Roger. He was in law school, and he looked just like Christian Bale, still in the pantheon in those days. At least he did to me, and my perception is the only one that matters in such matters, is it not? He had the eyes and the floppy hair, and the Van Dyke.

No one else seemed to see it, but the perceived resemblance made him incredibly hot to me. He thought I liked him because he was going to be a lawyer, make good money, would be quite the catch! Pfft! I didn't care about any of that.

The law is the biggest racket in the world, and I had my own money. But when we were in the dim bedroom together, that imagined resemblance was just enough to add a little extra spice to my enjoyment of the thing. More than the poor dear could've ever imagined, with his dull, lawyer's mind.

Right on schedule, Roger passed the bar. Then he shaved and got a haircut for his first day at his firm. His resemblance to Christian Bale quite disappeared then, washed down the drain, left on the barber's floor. And my affection went along with it, swept right away into the trash with those discarded locks. Imagine poor Roger's consternation at my sudden coldness. Oh, well. *It was a fine affair, mein Herr. But now it's over.* You are a stranger to me.

FOUR

How did I get to be this way, you ask? Serial obsessionist, shallow appreciator of a man only for his looks? Seriously not normal, you say? Possibly. But I like how I am. One never gets a broken heart if one only loves good-looking, famous men in that same fragile heart. A rich fantasy life is ever so much more rewarding than a mundane real life, going on boring dates with boring men, having ho-hum sex with ho-hum men. Pass.

But I am no ascetic. Every now and then, some everyman will catch my eye, if he has a passing resemblance to someone in the revered pantheon, as poor Roger did. But usually the resemblance fades as reality sets in, and then I just end it while the ending is still good. Before I begin to seriously dislike him.

I've never had to flat out tell any of them. "Look, I was only attracted to you in the first place because you reminded me of so-and-so," never had to actually draw them that picture.

But if he came upon me looking at pictures and said, "Who's that?"

I would reply, "Oh, that's so and so. You kinda remind me of him." And then sometimes I would be in the mood after reinforcing that resemblance in my head, and sometimes he would be able to make the connection.

Que sera, sera, whatever will be, will be - I find it to be a great life, and nobody ever gets hurt. At least *I* never get hurt. There is no harm in fantasizing about famous men. It is only when one tries to drag the fantasy into the real world that problems arise.

But how did I get this way, you insist? Most people prefer the real thing to anything that they can only think about, right? To this, I say that most people don't have my highly refined representational process. Like Paul Simon said, *If you took all the girls I knew when I was single/and brought them all together for one night/I know they'd never match my sweet imagination/and everything looks worse in black and white.*

There is never one thing undesirable about a fantasy man: in your mind, he's always on time, never says the wrong thing, and doesn't have stupid, boorish friends to whom he constantly subjects you. He doesn't play video games; he brings you gifts when gifts are appropriate. He always has plenty of money. He's fantastic in bed.

If this sounds crazy to you, I need to also tell you this. When I've found a new obsession, I walk around in a state of semi-arousal all day long. Just to allow the thought of the chosen one to pass through my mind will bring waves of fresh stimulation. This can go on for *months*. What real man can elicit that kind of state for that long?

But I must also clear up the difference between the agony of *unrequited* love - where you see the object every day at the office, say, or he's married to your sister - and *unrequitable* love - where you don't now know and will never actually meet the object. This difference is wide indeed. That thing that was left in the box - *hope* - that is what makes unrequited love hurt so much. The idea that there might be some ghost of a chance between you and him, some day, *somehow* - that hope is a killer. I experienced that hope about Benji - there was no logical reason why he and I shouldn't have been able to hook up. Other than the altogether unfortunate fact that he didn't want to. Sometimes hope sucks.

But *unrequitable* love! That's infinitely better. He's all you could ever want, even though you know that you'll never have him. That way, he can never disappoint you. Yet, still, you can think about him all day, think about how it would be. But since it will never be, there are never any accompanying anxieties about how you would actually go about pulling it off. No real life anxieties about what if (if you were to succeed in actually pulling it off) what if he doesn't like you, what if he thinks you're fat? What if he isn't any good? None of the disappointments of real love need ever intrude into the fantasy of unrequitable love.

However, I must note that on occasion a problem has been known to arise with the fantasy life, the obsessionist life. It is really just a tiny, teensy-weensy problem, but it must be mentioned.

Every now and again, you see, one loses control. The lofty ideals of unrequitable love collide with the base hope of unrequited love. One actually starts to hope that hope - what if I *could* actually meet him? And that can never happen, because even if, by some extraordinary coincidence, you were to run into him coming out of some restaurant on Sunset Boulevard, there would still be that fan-friend gulf, that divide not to be bridged. Even if you could somehow manage to approach him on the street, he would still know you for *one of them.*

When you start to feel that desire - when you start to formulate concrete, doable plans to actually in-person meet the obsession, warning bells should go off. This is a dangerous desire. *Trust me.* I would say that it's something to be exorcised immediately when it occurs - but once it occurs, you don't want to exorcise it. *All you want to do is to meet him.* And sometimes the lengths that you will go to, well . . . They can be lengthy, indeed.

FIVE

But okay, you want a little back-story on me. I am an only child, the only kind to be. I was the apple of Mom and Dad's eye, as all only children are. I never had a shadow of a doubt that I was the most important thing to them, never doubted that I was unconditionally loved, that I was the favorite.

Roger used to complain about being the middle child. He'd whine that, growing up, he was always too young - and Mom and Dad chose his big brother instead - or he was too old and they chose his younger sister. I would reply, "I feel your pain, Bra, but I just can't relate."

Mom worked at a law firm, and while she wasn'st an attorney, you wouldn't have guessed it by looking at her. Think of Joan from *Mad Men*, but just a little more modern and considerably more conservative.

She appreciated fine art. I dog-eared all her coffee table books of the great masters when I was a kid, fascinated with the colors and the shapes. She had a collection of records entitled *Living Shakespeare*, which she played for me, instilling an appreciation that I carry to this day. I remember the voices, the sound effects swelling out of the huge console hi-fi in the living room. (That's *hi-fi*, not *Wi-Fi*, kids. Google it.)

She played these records for me almost from birth. One of the favorite family stories went that Dad would come in and I would be in the playpen and *Julius Caesar* would be playing in the background. He'd tell my mom, "She can't understand that, you know."

And my mom would smile and reply, "Oh, but she will." Mom also used to love to tell people that I would get frightened and hide under my blanket when the ghost of Hamlet's father would make his entrance.

Surely better fare for the imagination, certainly better for my soul than *Little Red Riding Hood* and *Three Billy Goats Gruff.*

When I was a kid, Mom tried to teach me how to wear makeup and comport myself like a lady, but I was Daddy's little tomboy. Dad was a mechanic, owned his own shop. I learned everything that there was to know about cars almost before I learned to walk. I could tune your engine like Junior's crew chief, and change your tires almost as fast as his crew, by the time I was twelve. Brakes were my favorite, though. All that essential negative power at one's fingertips, all the safety of life and limb dependent on a couple of vulnerable hydraulic lines, some fittings; a couple of diaphragms and a tiny reservoir of precious fluid.

Although I never was allowed to work on customers' cars in an official getting-paid-for-it capacity (I was just a kid, after all), Dad loved to show off my skill and knowledge to his friends, having them play ask-me-anything about whichever make and model they chose.

Mom didn't care for this game. She referred to these demonstrations at the shop as him *treating me as his dancing monkey*. But I loved it.

Dad was also an outdoorsman, a hunter. He drew the line at actually taking me hunting with him, however, saying that there was too much rough talk and his buddies taking a pee behind a bush. It was no place for his little girl, he said. Years later, Mom would tell me that Dad didn't want to take me along because she had a suspicion that Dad wasn't really out bagging rabbits on all those winter weekends. She had an inkling that he might've been visiting a woman on the side, when he was supposed to be out hunting.

By the time Mom told me these revelations, Dad was gone, the victim of a freak accident at the shop, wherein some lady's Buick slid off the rack and crushed him.

But even if he would never take me out to actually kill things, Dad did teach me how to shoot. He taught me that a gun is a tool, just like a hammer. Except a gun is a tool for killing things, and thereby had to be treated with a certain kind of respect. He used to smile and say, "You *could* kill someone with a hammer, I guess, but this .45 is actually designed for it. And thereby, far more efficient."

"Why do you have so many guns, Dad?" I used to like to ask him.

It never failed to make me smile when he would reply, "So I'm ready for the uprising."

Like with everything else Dad taught me how to do, I excelled at shooting. I could keep up with all his buddies shooting skeet, and no beer bottle was safe on a fence when I had a rifle in my hand, no menacing bad guy target was gonna make it out of the range alive if I was holding a pistol. There was not a weapon he owned that I couldn't take apart and put back together, blindfolded.

And he had quite the collection: pistols, rifles, shotguns, a sweet FN FAL that he taught me to shoot as soon as I was big enough that it wouldn't knock me down. I used to come back from the range looking like somebody beat me: my shoulder all black and blue from the kick of that FAL. But it seemed nothing but smooth to me.

My mother sold the FAL not long after Dad died. She said that it was like having a howitzer in the house. When I told her that a howitzer was a piece of field artillery, she then said it reminded her of news clips she'd seen of the guy holding up the gun that killed Kennedy. When I told her that the gun that killed Kennedy was an Italian gun, and this was a German gun, and that they were only similar in that they were both, indeed, *guns*, she told me that it wasn't ladylike to know so much about firearms, and sold it anyway.

When I cried and said that I didn't have anything to remember Dad by except for his guns, she said, "And the money from his life insurance." But she didn't sell any more of his guns.

Once Dad was gone (I'd just turned thirteen), I began to listen to Mom more about all the ladylike business. Once Dad wasn't around for me to impress anymore, I turned my attention to impressing Mom. I dutifully went to ballroom dancing lessons in middle school and excelled at them. I ignored my friends and listened to my mother about how to apply makeup, how to dress. And nothing impressed her more than to see me dressed to the teeth.

So from Dad I learned about cars and guns, and from my mom, I learned how to comport myself like a lady, how to dress and snare a man. At least, *I think* she was trying to teach me about men. After Dad died, Mom would get in her cups sometimes. Then she'd play Grandma's Frank Sinatra records and regale me with stories of her boyfriends before Dad, how she'd learned at an early age that men would lie and cheat. She wanted me to know what steps to take to avoid these betrayals. I was only thirteen or fourteen at the time, so the lessons really went over my head.

SIX

So now that we've come back around to men again, perhaps you're wondering if there is something in my history on that account that might lend an explanation to my odd . . . *hobby*. Perhaps. You be the judge.

My first boyfriend, if you could call him that . . . Let me start over. The first time I was ever in love was with a guy name DJ. Unfortunately, I can't remember if the D stood for Don or Dan. Or maybe it was Dave. I tried to remember his last name the other day, and came up with DJ Tanner. But that wasn't it. That was the name of one of the little girls on *Full House*. Then I thought that maybe his last name was Johnson. That had a little melodic quality to it: *DJ Johnson*. That was probably it.

Yes. Before Jeff, before Christian, before the boys in the band – before *anybody*, there had been DJ.

It was summertime and I was fifteen. Was life ever more wonderful than when you were fifteen and it was summertime? My mother had sent me out to get milk. As I walked by the parking lot of the grocery store, my attention was arrested by a nearly flawless 1969 Dodge Charger parked therein. Yes, my brothers and only friends, just like the General Lee from *The Dukes of Hazzard*. Except this one was green, that glorious Mopar green. The hood was open and a young man was peering into the engine compartment.

I stood there and just looked at him for some time. It was as if I'd never seen another human being before this moment, so strange and wonderful did he seem to me. He had both arms up, wrists casually laid against either side of the point of the hood. He drummed his fingers in the air. He was wearing faded jeans and cowboy boots, and a dark green t-shirt (almost the same color as his Dodge) with the sleeves cut off. His straight, longish hair was the color of wet straw, and the muscles in his arms reminded me of a statue of some ancient Greek athlete.

Never before in my short life had I ever noticed anyone, *anything,* like I noticed this boy. Perhaps this is a clue for you to my later obsessions: I feel the same way when a new object strikes my fancy, the same way I did when I saw DJ standing there looking at his engine. I stopped walking and just looked at him, all other errands, all other tasks, forgotten. He was the most fascinating thing I'd ever seen, and I thought, *Who is this?*

He undoubtedly was able to feel my continued open-mouthed stare, and after what seemed like several minutes of standing there, he finally turned around and looked at me. He had a thin, soft mouth, a patrician nose dusted with freckles, and the most incredible pale green eyes I have ever seen. His eyes were like a color that you might find on a calico cat: just the most extraordinary shade of light green.

If I search the Hollywood pantheon for the rest of my life (and I mostly have), I'll never find another man that looked like DJ. He was, I would find out, all of seventeen. I was dumbstruck at his beauty. *Fucking dumbstruck.*

My dumbfounded expression led him to crook up one corner of his mouth in a sly half smile. "Hi, there, Girlie," he said. "You know anything about cars?"

If he would've asked me anything else, I probably would've been unable to answer, unable to speak, as I'd be with Benji a lifetime later. I would've just stood there and stared at him. But here was a question that I could inescapably answer in the affirmative, and it snapped me immediately out of my teenage reverie.

"As a matter of fact, I do," I replied, feeling like a character in a movie at the cliché. I walked over to him and his car. He was a good nine inches taller than me. I looked up into those glorious, jade colored eyes and said, "What seems to be the problem?"

He was surprised at my response, but couldn't deny my confidence. "It starts, but then it won't go."

I stood on the bumper and took the air cleaner off. I poked around for a minute and discovered that the throttle linkage was broken. I jumped off the bumper and looked around on the ground until I found a little piece of wire. I climbed back up on the bumper and used it to tie up the crippled linkage. I put the air cleaner back on and jumped down again, slammed the hood.

"Try it now."

Without a word, DJ did as he was bid. The Charger rumbled to fossil-fuel-sucking life when he turned it over, and my MacGyver repair held when he revved it up. He shut it down again and got out of it and just stood there looking at me for a minute, his arms crossed across his chest.

Now I smiled. "You're going to have to get that properly repaired. That wire won't last forever."

He still just looked at me with those fantastic green eyes. I felt like my heart had stopped and that I might fall over any minute; the summer afternoon had suddenly grown quite oppressively hot. Finally he said, "Can I give you a ride anywhere, Girlie?"

The admonitions every child has heard about getting into cars with strangers played through my mind and then dissipated into the heat like so much humidity. I told him that I had to go in and get some milk, and then he could give me a ride home, if that was okay. I retrieved the milk and got in the car without a split second of hesitation.

Something was rolling around in a small toolbox in the backseat. I said, "I might've been able to fix it permanently if you'd told me that you had tools."

"That's my brother's," he said. "I don't even know what's in there."

Curious now, I reached over the seat and flipped open the lid on the tool box. There was a flat head screwdriver, a pair of channel locks, a Crescent wrench, and a beefy pair of dikes, none of which would've been much help with fixing the linkage. I shut the toolbox.

"The door on the passenger side won't lock, either," he said. "Can you fix that?"

I smiled. "Not with what you have in that toolbox."

SEVEN

He waited in the driveway while I took the milk into the house, and when my mom asked where I was going now, I told her that I was going to the park with a friend from school. She told me to be back before nine, and then I was back inside that immaculate Charger with my perfect knight.

We drove to the park, which was the place to go if you were a kid with wheels, and in gratitude for my off-the-cuff repairs, he let me drive the Charger around in the parking lot. Back in the day, as the kids say now, back in the day (before they were born), the coolest thing was to have house speakers sitting on the deck above the backseat of your car. You'd have them on really long wires, so you could take them out and set them on the roof of the car and blast the tunes. The problem with this set up was that if you stopped too fast, sometimes the speakers would fly forward and hit you in the back of the head, but that was a small price to pay for so much coolness. Or at least, I thought so. Give me a break, I was fifteen.

DJ put his speakers on the roof and put some mellow tape in, and the sun went down and we sat on the hood of the car, leaned against the windshield and stared up at the sky. We talked, but I cannot for the life of me recall what it was we talked about. He asked me if I wanted a Kool, and I said, "Sure, I'll give it a try."

When he put his arm around me, I flinched like a rabbit, prompting him to again ask me how old I was.

I reiterated that I was fifteen, and he told me to relax, and after a second I snuggled against him and let him put his arm around me. The night was humid, hot, like the air in the bathroom when you step out of the shower. I could smell all of DJ's smells: cigarettes; the cotton of his t-shirt, the tang of some aftershave, the warm, sweet smell of his body, so different and beguiling. I was probably more aroused at that moment that I would be again for *years*, but I was too young to know it.

After a moment, DJ leaned over and kissed me, slowly, gently, and I didn't flinch this time. It was the most wondrous thing that had happened to me in my tiny little life, and after a few seconds I began to kiss him back. I mean, I *really* kissed him back, crawling over and lying on top of him, pinning him to the Charger's windshield. This was the greatest thing ever!

It was a good thing that he was almost as young as I was, and didn't realize the power of his kisses, didn't realize that I would've done anything he asked at that moment. I would've killed someone for him if he would've but nodded. I would've taken off all my clothes and gleefully climbed in the back seat of that green Dodge if he would've asked me to, without a backward glance. Just to see what was gonna happen next.

But he didn't ask me. We kissed some more and then he consulted his watch and said we had to go if I was going to make it home by nine. He jumped off the hood and then came around the other side, my knight, and pulled me off into his heavenly embrace. I was enveloped in his delicious, *different* smell, and when he kissed me - again, I would've done anything he asked. I was just that delighted with being kissed for the very first time. The word *ripe* comes to mind.

But all he asked me was to go to the movies with him the next night, and I agreed, happy, entranced beyond belief. He insisted on getting to the theater early, so that we could get the right seats.

The right seats, DJ explained, were three rows from the front and eight seats in. This was the best place in the theater for optimum sound quality, he said. I felt like I was looking up at the screen at a weird angle, but it didn't really matter to me anyway, because as soon as the lights went down I started to kiss him. This lasted through the previews, but when the feature started, he gently told me that we could do all this later. He wanted to watch the movie. I satisfied myself with holding hands with him.

On the way out of the theater, DJ noticed that some movie would be premiering the following weekend. For the life of me, I can't remember what the movie was. All I can remember is that he was very excited that it was coming out, that he couldn't wait to see it.

I saw him every day the following week. We hung out at the park, smoked Kools. We tossed a Frisbee once, listened to music, and made out. He didn't attempt any improprieties with me; he remained blissfully unaware of my willingness. We just kissed a lot, rolling around on the hood of his car, in the backseat, in the grass.

On Thursday, I mentioned something about that movie he'd said he'd wanted to see. He said he'd call me the next day about it. He had to help his brother move or something, and he said that he'd call me when he was done.

But he didn't call. I waited and waited, devastated, wondering, fearing that something terrible had happened to him. Maybe my rigged throttle linkage had failed as he tried to cross a railroad track. Maybe he'd fallen down a flight of steps and a couch had landed on his head while he was helping his brother.

Mom was utterly unaware that any change had taken place in her baby girl. She didn't see that I was no longer a selfish child, but was now someone who cared for someone else more than myself. She didn't know that I'd caught the eternal disease, that I was now in thrall to a cruel and insane master. She didn't realize that I was in the throes of my very first love. She knew that I liked the boy with the green car, but she had no idea that I loved him to the height and depth and breadth my soul could reach.

When he had not called by eight, she suggested that we go out for ice cream, because I hadn't been out of the house all day.

The ice cream place was across the square from the theater, and halfway through a banana split that tasted like cold, lumpy sand, I noticed DJ's Dodge in the parking lot. There was no mistaking it.

"Oh, look, Mom! There's Penny in line at the movies!" Penny was a girl from school, and she'd been away all summer at camp; I'd longed for her return, so I could tell her all about DJ.

My mother sighed. "Here's ten dollars," she said, rooting around in her purse. "Call me if you need a ride home."

I thanked her and dashed across the street and got in line. I stood close to a stranger that looked like Penny. But it wasn't Penny; she was still at summer camp. I'd conjured Penny out of thin air when I'd spied DJ's Charger. I couldn't think past the idea that he was in the theater and I wanted to be in there with him.

The movie that he'd wanted to see had already started. I bought a ticket to something else, and then snuck into the theater. I didn't have to fumble around in the dark looking for him, either. I knew exactly where he would be: three rows back and eight seats in. I stalked down the aisle, excited at the prospect of surprising him, telling myself that he hadn't called because he didn't want me pawing him during this movie that he so wanted to see.

But as I approached the row, the scene in the film brightened considerably, and the surprise was most assuredly on me. There he was in his accustomed seat, but he was not alone. He was locked in torrid embrace with a blonde. One hand raced through her hair, the other groped eagerly at her ample breast. There was more petting going on than he'd ever tried with me. The scene darkened mercifully, and I fled up the aisle.

I leaned against the side of the theater, away from the blinking lights of the marquee, and tried to catch my breath. Again I felt that my heart had stopped, that I might fall over, but no longer in a good way. In fact, I thought that I might die, actually wished for it, that I might just drop dead right there in the parking lot. I begged God to make this pain end.

Sure, it was melodramatic, but I was only fifteen, and one feels everything so completely when one is fifteen. Finally, I caught my breath, looked around to see if anybody had noticed me hyperventilating beside the theater. No one had. The night went on as if my heart had not just been crushed.

I'd experienced my first true love as well as my first taste of jealousy, all in the same week. My face felt too hot; my head filled with white noise at the betrayal that I'd just endured. I'd loved DJ completely, with everything I had, because it was the first time I'd ever experienced love. Now all those glorious feelings were gone. He had taken them away. He was in there giving them to that fat-titted blonde.

Then the singing in my nerves ceased, but my mind was still hot, stuffed with deceptively cold-looking white ash. The embers glowed there just below the surface; the embers of a never-before felt hatred, the dark side of the never-before felt love I'd so recently discovered.

I looked at his Dodge in the parking lot; the grill seemed to grin at me. I hadn't even had the chance to fix that passenger side lock for him.

After what seemed like a lifetime, I walked away from his car, away from the flashing marquee.

Instead of calling my mother for a ride, I decided to walk home, clear my head. I blended into the darkness. When I got home, my mother called, "How was the movie?" as I ran up the stairs to my room. I told her it was great, and closed the door, and proceeded to cry myself immediately to sleep.

But despite how it might come across in the telling, DJ's betrayal didn't break my heart in such a way that I was damaged forever. I didn't become sullen or afraid, didn't become a hater of men. Me? Are you kidding? *Hot damn*, no one likes men more than me.

But I do think that his betrayal did put a crack in my heart. It wasn't a big crack, and it has healed over and been forgotten. It didn't even really leave a scar. But when DJ cracked my heart, something escaped. A great deal of my capacity to feel love for an actual flesh and blood man got away. My capacity to encompass it again in the way that I had for him just leaked out, not to be regenerated until just recently.

I would feel attraction and lust, of course, and even affection again in real life. But whatever the ephemera was, the essence that was necessary to experience those feelings of *just simple love* for someone that was actually standing there looking at me? That was mostly gone.

I would know a great many men in my life (as I said, who likes men more than me?), and I liked them all well enough. But I would never experience, tried to never *let myself experience*, that sublime aching love again, like that first love that I'd felt for DJ. Not in real life. And, by God, I did succeed for a long time in not feeling it. But in the end that same kind of aching love in real life would overtake me, and I would be buried completely by it.

As far as the fantasy men are concerned, however - throughout this confessional, if you find my descriptions of the perfection of these objects to be purple and way too enthusiastic for a grown woman, I'm sorry, but I'm *not sorry*. There's no feeling in the world as wonderful as that first blush of excitement that you feel when you are attracted to someone.

I'm a good twenty years gone from being a teenager. But I remember what it was like to be young and flushed with love. I remember what it was like when the cherished one blotted out all other thoughts in my mind. When the very idea of him filled me completely with that warm bliss.

Do you remember what it was like? Wasn't it bitchin', to feel so alive? I've retained the ability to still feel that complete infatuation knifing through my soul (in a good way). Can you still do that? Or has life and reality, time and just plain disappointment dulled your ability to feel that teenage kind of longing ever again? I feel sorry for you, because I can still summon it up, as easily as looking at a photograph. It's just not there for anyone I actually know.

But if the sometimes adolescent quality of my praises offends you, you can just eat your heart out and deal with all my gushing appreciation. Because it's as real to me at thirty-five as it ever was at fifteen, makes me feel just that alive, every time. Even if the men themselves aren't real.

Anyway, back to DJ.

A sad story, you say? Sad, but common. I did eventually forget completely about DJ, as is evidenced by my inability to remember any details, such as what his name was exactly. All I can remember now is the way he looked. Those jade colored, light green eyes. I don't even remember the hurt anymore. All I remember now is the way he kissed, the way I would've died for him.

And his car. That sweet, green Charger.

I probably remember the car so clearly, because the next morning my mother came up to my room with tears in her eyes and the newspaper twisted in her hand. "Oh, God!" she wailed. "It could've been you!"

She threw the newspaper on the bed and clutched me to her, and over her shoulder I saw the picture. The grainy black and white made it hard to make out, not to mention the carnage of the wreck itself. *Two die in collision with tree*, the small headline stated in its small way. I didn't need to read the details - maybe I'd remember his name now, if I/d read the details. I recognized the Dodge.

But my mom had read it, and that was why she was hugging me to her and moaning about how it could've been me. DJ was dead, and apparently the blonde was too. I felt numb. My mother was crying and telling me how sorry she was that my friend was killed, without ever realizing how much more he'd been to me than just a friend. She'd never know that he'd been my first true love, the first one (the only one, really) that I'd allowed in enough to break my heart.

EIGHT

I went out on my fair share of dates in high school. I did a lot of making out (I've always really enjoyed kissing), did a little petting. And I enjoyed it all immensely, don't get me wrong. But none of my peers, panting heavily in my ear and begging, "Oh, baby, come on, please!" ever engendered that desire to shuck my clothes and find out what comes next the way DJ did.

So I was untried when I met Harry at the self-same park where I'd once parked with poor, dead DJ and smoked Kools and listened to tunes and innocently made out. Perhaps that isn't an exact statement, because certainly, many had tried. Say instead that I was *unachieved* when I met Harry.

Harry was my forbidden love. He was ten years older than me, and I liked to say he was a poor girl's Tom Selleck. I'll never forget the first time I saw him playing Frisbee in the sun. He had the dimples, and the shaggy hair and the mustache, but not the blue eyes. He was the first grown man who'd ever looked twice at me. I was seventeen when we met.

From a physical, blooming-of-womanhood standpoint, what I liked about Harry was the same thing I'd liked about DJ. I had loved to just kiss DJ, and he never (the poor, dead thing) had ever suggested anything that I wouldn't have done. Harry was the same, in that I could kiss him and hold his hand and put my head on his chest and my hand on his knee, any familiarity that I desired, and he let me just go along and do it at my own pace. Contrast this to my heavy-breathing peers who were always pushing and pushing, wheedling and cajoling, begging and demanding. If you squeezed one of their hands too tightly, he thought that it was a signal that you were ready for the main event.

And then it was always a struggle, always a little bit of pleasure followed by an entire evening of slapping hands away and saying no. It was tiresome. But with Harry, it was all different, because he was older and calmer and just let me go at my own pace.

This approach of his, in hardly any time at all, led to the following exchange:

Breathlessly, like a character from a romance novel, my overheated virgin self breathed, "I want you to do it now, Harry! I want to do it *now*!"

"Are you sure?"

"Yes! *Yes!* I am *absolutely sure!*"

"Okay."

Harry went right on ahead and did what I'd begged him to do, and I must say that it was awesomely everything I'd ever thought it might be, yet, on the same note, I couldn't understand what the big deal about *not* doing it had been. In other words, it didn't seem like such a big deal to do this lovely, lovely thing, and I wondered why I hadn't been doing it sooner.

And the experience with Harry contributed a little to the obsession format, I guess. Because, surely, there is no man sexier than the one that gets you so wound up that you would beg him to do you. I would've begged Jeff for it, and Christian, and Benji.

Harry only possessed the power to make me beg for it that one time, sadly. Just that one time, *the first time*. After that, I was again in control.

That more-than-willing-to-beg-for-it train would eventually pull back into my station again, however, and another man would step off of it, a perfect man. And he would smile at me . . .

NINE

Anyway.

My mom decided that she had to put the kibosh on the whole impossible thing with Harry, once she overheard me talking to him on the phone one night, making plans to head to Oregon with him, to find a cabin and live off the land, or some other clap trap like that.

Three days after she overheard this conversation, Harry called and insisted that I come out and meet him at the local Denny's. It was a strange request, because he usually came over to my house and picked me up, but I complied.

When I arrived, I found that Harry had changed his appearance. Like Roger, years later, Harry had shaved and gotten a haircut, and the resemblance to Tom Selleck had disappeared with his mustache. In fact, Harry had an upper lip like a chimpanzee, once he had no mustache. I looked at him, unable to hide my sudden distaste. The enjoyment of his looks, the attraction that had once made me beg him was immediately and irrevocably gone.

"Why the cloak and dagger?" I asked. "Did you want to surprise me with your . . . Your new look?"

"A private detective stopped by my office today." He slid a business card across the table toward me. I recognized the name on the card. It was my "Uncle" Freddy, one of my mom's co-workers. I guessed what was coming next. "Apparently, your mother sent him by to tell me that if I don't stop seeing you, she'll have me arrested for statutory rape."

I would've objected, would've defied my mother, gone on the lam and run off to the wilds of Oregon with him. If only he hadn't shaved. Now I just took in the new, plain man, monkey lip and all, and shrugged. "Maybe it's for the best."

High school graduation loomed, and I hadn't formulated any ideas for what I'd do next. Those Oregon plans had been there in my head, but after Harry never called again (thank Christ), those thoughts disappeared, too. Maybe I might want to go to college, but didn't have an inkling of what I wanted to be.

Mom came to the rescue. She sat me down one evening not long after my expedition to Denny's. She explained that I had to stop thinking that Prince Statutory Rape Charming was going to ride into town and whisk me off to parts unknown, and then I'd have a life all made up for me. I'd have to make my own way, she said.

"What do you think of my job?" she asked, but she already knew the answer. My mom was an executive secretary, and I was proud of her. She got up every morning and went to work, flawlessly turned out in her business suit. Numerous attorneys had praised her competence, her indispensability to me at all the many office Christmas parties that I'd been attending with her since I was a child.

"I would love to work at your office," I replied.

She smiled and produced a college catalog, voila! as if out of thin air. I wouldn't even have to leave town, could take all the classes for my paralegal at the community college. If I might've had higher ambitions, Mom didn't ask about them. Since I didn't, I didn't bring them up either. Aspiring to be a paralegal was already several rungs up the ladder from executive secretary, and that was high enough up for both of us.

TEN

And so it was decided, and I never looked back.

I had the best of all possible worlds during college. I didn't have to worry about paying the tuition (Dad's life insurance had taken care of all that), so I didn't have to get a job. I got to live at home, rent free. Mom gave me all the money I needed for expenses. She viewed me as a responsible adult, now that I was getting my life in order, so she didn't get all parental on me if I occasionally stayed out all night.

The Benji thing happened during those days: I drove all over the state every weekend for a year, missing football games and other school related extra-curricular activities. I met, dated, seduced and also subsequently dumped Roger during my last year in college.

But during those glorious days of freedom and experimentation, there were other forays into real life besides just Roger. My imagination is such that I didn't have to go too far off the beaten track into reality, but let's just say that I participated enough, got enough actual experience under my belt to learn exactly what I liked. No one is more able to recognize the triggers of desire than me. Never do I have to wonder what it is that I find attractive about someone. Physically, I like them taller than me, broad-shouldered and slender. I had a blonde phase for a moment, there in college; for a month or so, I would even look twice at an ugly blonde. But it passed.

Regardless of their hair color, in my mind, I often supplied a personality for the men I dated in real life, because I wasn't going to be around long enough to find out what they were actually like. I undoubtedly dreamt them to be nicer than they really were, smarter, sharper. It was all harmless fun.

ELEVEN

Mom finagled me a position at her firm, and I started the Monday after graduation. Since that day, I've worked my way up, paid my dues, any cliché you like. At thirty-five, I am the youngest head paralegal they've ever had.

There's not much more to tell about my life, up to the point where everything changed. For the first five years that I worked there, there were just too many late nights at the office, too many classes to take, too many certifications to master. *No time for love, Dr. Jones.* Just like while I was in college, I still got my licks in, so to speak. I went out enough - one cannot live by pictures alone. But enough for me would've been seldom indeed for most. There were never any prospects worth more than two or three encounters.

From the first day I started working there, Mom had sternly forbidden me from dating anyone at the firm. Not just the firm - she forbade me from seeing anyone that even worked in the building. Young women so easily acquired a bad reputation, she said, and it was much better to be safe than sorry, career-wise. Her arguments all were sound and made perfect sense, and even after she retired, I saw no reason to violate her edicts. There was no one in the building that was attractive to me anyway; I noticed no one and no one noticed me.

Except for Charlie, of course. Charles J. Bakke, one of the junior partners. He noticed me. He was as boring a contract lawyer as there could be, shy and bookish. Charlie had quite the crush on me; it was obvious from his smiles and stammers. I was nothing but kind to him. I was never one to be so full of myself that I felt it necessary to be cruel to men that liked me, just because I felt nothing in return. Try as I might, though (it wasn't much), I could conjure up nothing for Charlie and gently declined any requests for dates that he managed to summon up the courage to propose. I was nice enough to him that he kept asking, and that was okay.

TWELVE

Before everything changed irrevocably, it had actually been several years since I'd found a good obsession. There were a few blips on the radar, but no one really caught my eye, struck my heart, pierced my loins, so to speak. Call them *obsessions lite*. I was ripe for a new, complete inundation of fantasy, a new preoccupation.

And then the celestial alignments occurred, and by beloved *Netflix* went to streaming.

Ah, *Netflix!* If video killed the radio star, then *Netflix* killed the video store. I read once that in the video rental biz you had *Blockbuster* on one side, and then you had all the other video rental stores in existence on the other and all of them put together didn't add up to *Blockbuster.*

Then *Netflix* came along with movies you would get through the mail! You'd never again have to get up off your fat ass and go to the video store, only to wander around and discover that they didn't have anything that you wanted to see.

I tried to remain loyal to *Blockbuster*. That deal they had, wherein you could take your mail movies and then trade them in at the store? That was marketing genius. But their mail service was just too damn expensive. *Blockbuster* had been blindsided by *Netflix*. First they were unwilling to compete (they were *fucking Blockbuster Video*, after all, for Christ's sake!) And then they were unable to compete. And then they went the way of the dodo.

Oh, the hours, the days, *the weeks* that I spent walking around in *Blockbuster* video and places just like it, searching for bad, limited release, straight to video movies! *RIP Blockbuster*, and all your smaller brethren, too. But I don't miss that driving all over town shit. Not one little bit.

The *Netflix* streaming made it so you didn't have to think at all. Didn't have to even think enough to pick out something that you might want to see and wait for it to come in the mail. With the streaming you could just sit there and drool on yourself, paging through every imaginable kind of movie, television, documentary. It is truly a wonderful time to be alive.

My first forays into *Netflix* streaming involved a couple Clive Owen movies. I even sat through some Zac Efron thing with Claire Danes and some other guy who did a spot-on Orson Welles. The movie itself was terrible, but he was brilliant in it, as was Zac.

It seemed that I was tending to lean toward dark-haired men with blue eyes in my thirty-five-year-old dotage. Clive struck me only partially, and while Zac was indeed dreamy, I was just a little too old to flip over him. I couldn't even bring myself to *begin* to endure that *High School Musical* thing. He would've been right up there, had he been around when I was twenty, but these days? Meh. Let's not be absolutely ridiculous.

THIRTEEN

It didn't take long for me to discover that the best thing or the worse thing about the *Netflix* streaming (depending on how you look at it) is that they don't often have a lot of new releases available to stream, but by God, they have tons of ancient, little known black and white movies; documentaries about damn near every facet of our wide, wide world; gazillions of really bad horror movies acted almost entirely by unknowns; and lots and lots of foreign shit.

As you may have surmised by this point, I love movies. Movies and music; although I must admit to a rather provincially mainstream taste in both. I have a knack for committing song lyrics and movie lines to memory, and something germane never fails to come to mind in everyday circumstances. Life is far more interesting when one can call up a famous observation, some clever commentary on any situation.

You can always tell a movie buff after just a short conversation. They will repeat some obscure line and when you don't get the reference, they'll ask you, "Don't you know what that's from?"

Where else do you find actors to obsess over, except in movies? Movies show up the boring reality of life; where else is everything so well lit, where else is there ever such apt music playing in the background? Who, in real life, speaks such catchy and memorable lines?

And I love television, too, of course, the ritual of looking forward all week to when the next episode of the beloved series would be on. But I got a little snobbish, almost from the first day they installed my cable, and vowed to never watch free TV again. So I missed a lot of great series in their entirety, just from being a snob. But I wasn't too snobbish that I paid for the premium cable channels either, so I also missed all of *Showtime* and *Cinemax's* offerings.

But once *Netflix* streaming started playing series that had been broadcast on free TV and premium cable, I had the best of both worlds. I could watch a whole season of something in a weekend. Commercial free.

So perhaps I can lay the blame on *Netflix*, if blame must indeed be laid. *Netflix* and their fucking foreign movies, their foreign television. I sincerely dislike subtitles, but if something looks good, I will suffer through them. *Dumplings* was completely awesome. I loved *Troll Hunter*, and that other Norwegian or Swedish or whatever one about the malevolent Santa Claus. All of these were worth the subtitles.

Then there was *The Beekeeper.* What's that? You say you don't remember *The Beekeeper*? It was on for three seasons ten years ago. The premise involved an entomologist (*a what?*), the youngest tenured professor at the university. He was also a master beekeeper, or whatever you call the local authority on bees.

His buddy was a forensic scientist at the same university, and the scientist's love interest was a cop, and they all solved crimes together. The cop and the forensic scientist turned to the beekeeper for help, because, you see, he was sort of Indiana Jones and Sherlock Holmes and MacGyver all rolled into one, with a little John Muir thrown in for some social and environmental preaching. He was always dropping Marcus Aurelius quotations, such as *everything we hear is an opinion, not a fact. Everything we see is a perspective, not the truth.*

The lady cop tolerated the forensic guy, but in reality, she had the hots for the beekeeper. Of course, the beekeeper was oblivious to her longings, mostly because he was just too damn Zen for all that earthy stuff. *The art of living is more like wrestling than dancing.*

So, as Fate would decree it, one night, I decided to give *The Beekeeper* a try. I was bored and the description sounded different. My uncle raises bees. I found it to be cute without being trite, sometimes even a little thought provoking without being overly preachy.

It had that element that made for the best cop shows: right when you were chuckling at some funny incident, right when you were thinking, *Hey, this is a pretty funny show*, they would drop something heavy on you, like blowing up one of the leads or having the guest star turn traitor or get murdered.

But most of the plot and the action were all highly unlikely. Since when did cops consult with bug doctors? I figured that would probably be as frowned upon as consulting with psychics.

Aren't most dramadies that way, though? If TV was like real life - ponderous, predictable, a place where the protagonist usually always loses - who would watch it? The happy ending, the exaction of a righteous and just revenge, the bad guys getting their deserved comeuppance - that suspension of disbelief is what it's all about.

One Jake Franklin played the title role, along with a cast of other equally unknowns. He wasn't in the first three episodes; although his name was on the cast list. The first three episodes were all exposition, building up to the introduction of his character - you just saw his character's name on his office door.

So it would take me exactly four episodes before I came to understand just exactly how devastating was Jake Franklin. And when the credits rolled, after Episode Four, Season One, I was hooked, as surely as any junkie who ever stuck a needle in his arm.

Oh, my God, he is breathtaking! *Who is this guy?*

He was the very apogee of my new fixation on dark-haired, blue eyed men. He was like the twins from the band, they of the black hair and pale skin, like milk. But there the resemblance ended, and there was their memory wiped irrevocably from my mind.

Yea, verily, the memory of every other obsession I'd ever had was disappeared after Episode Four of *The Beekeeper*. The memory of every other man that I'd known in real life, too. Gone. I became, in Madonna's words, *like a virgin*, upon beholding this Jake Franklin.

I can only describe him in superlatives. He was absolute, white-boy perfection. I would later find out that he was twenty-six at the start of the series; but he didn't look a day over nineteen. That was a running gag on the show, how young he looked, what with him being a professor and all.

He was tall, unlike the itty-bitty twins, broad shouldered, slender but sturdy. And unlike the twins' brown eyes (which suddenly seemed so muddy to me), Jake Franklin had enormous blue eyes. Eyes to simply die for. Were I a poet, I could write a sonnet to his eyes, of the deepest, darkest blue.

His teeth were just the slightest bit crooked, just crooked enough to be utterly delightful. Combined with the ripe, flawless mouth, his smile was enough to launch a thousand ships.

I was completely, instantaneously addicted, was I, to Jake Franklin.

It was a Friday, I remember distinctly, and so besotted was I, that I didn't pause after Episode Four to hit the internet, but watched the entire series, all three seasons of *The Beekeeper*, episode after episode, back to back. Then I fell into a deep sleep and dreamed of hives and fingerprints and police procedure. But I didn't dream of Jake Franklin, because that really would've been entirely too glorious.

The next morning, I arose refreshed and made myself a pot of coffee. While Saturday work was not unknown to our firm, mercifully, there was none on this Saturday, so I started off with Episode Four all over again.

His voice was low, deep; and despite the goody-two-shoes role and the Roman emperor quotations, I thought I could detect certain darkness in it. During one particularly long passage, I just closed my eyes and listened to him talk.

That was when I noticed the accent. It was subtle, something about the way he spoke his short vowels. There was something a little off about *not*. There it was again - the way he said *sore-y* instead of *sorry*. I opened my eyes. Where had I heard that accent before, that weird garbling of the o's, that unmistakably not-American way of saying *sore-y*?

And that was when the realization hit me that he was Canadian, they were all Canadian, it was a Canadian show. Fucking *Netflix* had sucked me in with their foreign shit. No wonder I had never seen this magnificent specimen of manhood before, why I'd never even *heard* of Jake Franklin. He was a Canadian.

How I'd missed all *The Beekeeper's* references to Alberta and Ontario and other obscure, totally foreign Canadian stuff before that, I'll never know. But it was the accent that I finally caught on to. *Sore-y.* Where had I heard that accent before? Who did I know that talked like that?

And then it hit me, and I snapped my fingers. Of course. Charles Bakke was Canadian. "*Sore-y* you couldn't make my New Year's Eve party." On Charlie, the accent was just one more thing that was annoying about him.

Still, I couldn't help wondering if he'd ever heard of his countryman, if he might have some Canadian anecdotes about Jake Franklin. So intrigued was I at discovering this vague connection, that I would have without hesitation called Charlie just to ask him if he'd ever heard of this guy, if I would've had Charlie's number.

I was a little embarrassed at the realization that I didn't. I'd known Charlie for all the years that I'd worked at the firm. We were co-workers, colleagues. *Friends,* even. I should've had Charlie's celly. I knew he'd asked for mine enough times.

It would just have to wait until Monday.

My reverie broken (*The Beekeeper* wasn't Shakespeare, after all), I decided to take a break from the viewing and hit the internet.

As befitting a Canadian, Jake's *Wikipedia* page was meager; four or five paragraphs at most, accompanied by as unflattering a picture as they could find of someone possessed of such godlike looks. From this paltry listing, it was confirmed that Jake Franklin (full name, *Jackson Alexander Franklin*) was indeed Canadian; he was now thirty-eight (a mere three years my senior).

The indefatigable *Wikipedia* delivered me the bad news: he'd been married for twenty long years to his high school sweetheart, whose name immediately slipped from my memory as water through a wide meshed sieve. They had no children. He'd done some modeling, some theater. *The Beekeeper* was his break-out role, the one that put him on the map in Canada (*and what a tiresomely big map it is,* I thought). The show had been an incredible hit in its day; he'd been one of the highest paid actors in Canadian television history during the last season.

Wikipedia devoted one whole paragraph to his tireless activism on behalf of the Canadian beekeeping community. It talked about how he was always petitioning the government, appearing at public hearings and all that, demanding that something be done about the Colony Collapse problems in Canada. It mentioned that he'd appeared in a documentary about the disorder, in character as *The Beekeeper.* I clicked on the link for the show and found that its article was five times as long as the one for the star, but I didn't read it then.

Fuck you, *Wikipedia.* Time to look for fan sites.

There were a few, and I stole all their pictures. They crowed (respectfully) of his wonderfulness, but they were all outdated, the links all broken and 404'ed: *The Beekeeper*, no matter how popular it'd once been, had been off the air for ten years. Apparently even his loyal Canadian fans couldn't keep up their enthusiasm for that long.

Except for one. The girl called herself *CanadaBees*, and had posted a picture and a comment to his glory *that very morning.* She had some 130 pages to her blog, each with five or six pictures of him, as well as commentaries with each. I immediately became one of her followers, and after spending the entire afternoon looking at her clever posts and stealing her awesome pictures, I sent her an email shamelessly praising her poetic soul and apt observations. I broke my own rule against ever contacting fan sites and exuberantly told her that while I was new to the amazing universe of Jackson Alexander Franklin, I would not have found it such a splendid place indeed had it not been for her site. She did not send a return email.

From *CanadaBees'* site, I learned that Jake's manager was his older brother, Greg, and that all fan mail and requests for autographed pictures should be sent to his attention at some weird address with too many rows and not enough commas in it, in some obscure Canadian town that I'd never heard of.

Here was a line I wouldn't cross; I didn't want any anonymously signed 8x10 glossies. Why would I, when *CanadaBees* had so kindly posted a copy of hers, as well as a zillion other pictures?

She had screen captures, publicity shots; even some old grainy shots of a very young Jake modeling clothes. She'd posted a full length picture of him playing Romeo (oh, that riot of black curls!), in doublet and hose, rapier and all, which I would've gladly had blown up and installed on my bedroom ceiling, had it not been for the fact that it was tiny and grainy and of no good resolution.

I clicked through the pages on her blog. Here was Jake at some kind of convention, standing next to older brother-manager Greg. I peered at him - he was attractive in his own right, although I didn't think they looked much like brothers. I was reminded of a line from that 1980's show, *Simon and Simon*, wherein Gerald McRaney and Jameson Parker (*who?*) played brothers who ran a detective agency. Noting that they didn't look like brothers, some character had said, "Different mother?" To which one of them replied, "Different mood."

In the shot *CanadaBees* had posted, Greg was looking at his brother over a pair of Ray-Bans, laughing. He had light blue-green eyes, dark brown but not quite black hair, cut in an excellent 'do, and a killer smile.

He was quite attractive, and I might have considered him twice, once upon a time, in that wasted epoch of the entirety of my life up to that point, *before Jake*. Now I would never consider anyone else, ever again.

Next *CanadaBees* provided us with a picture of Jake and his lovely wife (captioned *Canada's Most Fortunate Woman*), accompanied by her gushing thanks to said wife for so gamely putting up with all of her husband's crazy fan girls, with such good grace and all around wonderfulness. In the candid shot, the happy couple was smiling happily at one another, so obviously in love. She was shorter than him; gorgeous in the same healthy, fresh-faced way he was. I wondered, not for the last time, what the water must be like up there, that they all looked so glowing and robust. She was blonde and dimpled, with tiny, perfect, pearly teeth, and blue eyes almost the color of turquoise. I hated her utterly.

Some pages later, *CanadaBees* had posted another picture of them. This was a posed shot, taken from some article about the show that had appeared in some Canadian rag that I had, of course, never heard of. In this picture, they were both looking at the camera, not smiling, and the incredibly privileged Mrs. Franklin was standing in front of him protectively, as if saying, "Hands off, ladies. He's all mine." I noticed that *CanadaBees* hadn't added any gushingly grateful captions to *this* one.

So what if he was married, I thought to myself. At least he wasn't gay. When I found out that an obsession prospect was gay, the machine just automatically stopped. I couldn't fantasize about a man who didn't like women. I rather thought it wasn't my place, actually. If he was gay, then he was meant for the men to fantasize about.

Gay men were like devoted acolytes to a mysterious alien god to me. While thinking about what they did together might give me a momentary erotic pause - after all, the only thing better than one attractive man was two – in the end, I always felt like, if he was gay, then he wasn't for me, wasn't for women, and that I was being greedy if I obsessed on him for very long. Besides, there were more than enough straight men.

Jackson Alexander Franklin wasn't gay, was happily married. So he wasn't a serial womanizer like Bradley Cooper, he of the light blue eyes and the impossibly perfect teeth and the player's smile. I'd toyed with the idea of obsessing on Bradley at one time, after *The A-Team* came out. But now, just like everyone else, his star had been permanently eclipsed by everything embodied in my mind by those three little words: *Jackson Alexander Franklin.*

FOURTEEN

On Monday morning, I waited with no little impatience for Charlie Bakke to make his daily pilgrimage to my office to say hello. Soon enough, he appeared and asked me in his backward, sheepish way how I was, if I'd had a nice weekend.

You have no idea, I thought. But I said, "Say, Charlie, you're from Canada, right? Have you ever heard of an actor named Jake Franklin? I caught a couple episodes of *The Beekeeper* on *Netflix* over the weekend, and . . ."

But Charlie was laughing at me, that high, nasal, annoying, lawyer's horselaugh of his. Finally, he noticed that I was just staring at him and he abruptly ceased yukking it up. He said, "You're kidding, right?" When I just looked at him, blinking, he said, "Have I ever heard of Jake Franklin? I should think so. I was at his wedding. He's married to my sister."

The room started to spin then, my brothers and only friends, and it was a good thing that I was already sitting down. I felt my mouth drop open and had to make a conscious effort to snap it shut again.

Charlie continued, "As a matter of fact, I'm about to be his lawyer, too. He's going to be doing some new movie here in the States and he's retained us to negotiate the contract with the studio. That kind of thing's a lot more complicated here than in Canada. He and Sheila are coming down to stay with me in a few months, at least until they find some place in LA. Why do you ask?"

I gulped a lungful of air and lamely repeated, "I caught a couple episodes of *The Beekeeper* over the weekend. My . . . My uncle keeps bees and I've always found them . . . interesting."

"Oh, yeah. *Jake Franklin, the Face of Canadian Beekeeping.*" Mercifully, Charlie hadn't noticed my sudden and complete descent into disbelief. "I didn't know you were into bees. Would you like to meet him?"

So cavalier, so easy, so nothing to it. *Would you like to meet him? Would you like to meet the man of your dreams?* I struggled to maintain some semblance of a normal face. "S-S-Sure," I said, trying to be casual, failing miserably.

But Charlie didn't notice. "I'll have you over for dinner as soon as they're settled in here. He loves to talk to people about the bees."

I saw realization dawn in Charlie's eyes, but it wasn't any realization that I had to fear. He hadn't suddenly gleaned that I was completely besotted with his brother-in-law. No. What Charlie was suddenly realizing was the idea that I'd finally be coming over to his house, would finally be having dinner with him. His sister and brother-in-law were forgotten. It was all about us now, about what things might come for *him*, with *me*, out of this most serendipitous and coincidental situation.

His sad little lust helped me to recover my wits. "It's a date then," I said and smiled seductively at him. But just a little bit. I suddenly perceived vast and untapped uses for Charles J. Bakke, Attorney at Law.

"I'll let you know when they arrive," he said.

The phone on my desk rang at that moment, and I nodded at him, all business now, and answered it. Another partner walked up to the open door to my office and spoke to him. He waved goodbye to me, and the two of them left together.

I got off the phone as quickly as possible, arose unsteadily from my desk. I practically ran to the ladies lounge, and collapsed on the recliner that we kept in there, specifically for the break time comfort of our pregnant employees.

I couldn't catch my breath. This wasn't happening. I was going to get to meet Jackson Alexander Franklin? It defied all belief. It was a small world after all, I thought for a second, and then again the disbelief washed over me. This couldn't be real. I had to be dreaming. I pinched myself, actually *pinched* myself, to make sure I wasn't dreaming.

I was awake. This was no dream. I felt like the girl in *National Velvet*, that love story to the dearest desire of every fourteen-year-old city girl: horses. And she achieves everything her little heart desires, wins Piebald and the Grand National, all of it just an impossible dream at the beginning of the story.

But none of what happened to Velvet was as far-fetched as the idea of me actually getting to meet Jake Franklin. A half hour ago, *I* had more chance of winning the Grand National then of ever meeting Jake Franklin.

But it was no dream. Charlie Bakke's sister - what was her name again - Sandra? Shelly? Why could I not remember her name? Charles Bakke's sister was married to the most beautiful man in the world. And he was going to be here, *under my battlements*, in two short months. And I was going to get to meet him.

And it wouldn't be after standing in line in the rain at some convention. It wouldn't be as fan to famous. It would be as equals, as friends. We were going to talk about bees. Then came the panic: *what did I know about bees?* I sat there and panted.

One of the senior partners' executive secretaries came in, saw me there all aflutter, expressed concern. "Are you okay, honey? You don't look so hot," she said, sounding just like the secretary from *The Maltese Falcon*, the same kind of dame that she'd probably been in her youth. I smiled at the image, but still couldn't speak, just looked up at her, panting. "Looks like you're having a little panic attack. This place will certainly do it to ya. Nothing to worry about. Would you like a Valium?"

I nodded gratefully. She dug an amber colored medicine bottle out of her purse, and fished a pill out of it for me with a long scarlet fingernail. She put it in the center of my grateful palm and I dry swallowed it, eliciting a wince from her. Finally, my breathing started evening out. "Thank you," I gasped out.

"No problem, honey. Everybody needs a little calming sometimes. You just sit in here until you catch your breath, and in about twenty minutes, a visit from the president won't faze you."

FIFTEEN

The secretary was right. Twenty minutes later, I was as cool as the oft-mentioned cucumber, as mellow as a stoner on April 20th. Plots was I plotting. Work forgotten for the day, I was making out lists in a red steno pad. *Call Uncle Pete. Get some bees. Study up on bees. What do they eat in Canada? Get some of whatever it is.*

I'd completely forgotten the difference between unrequited and unrequitable. Jackson Alexander Franklin had been discovered, adored, desired and unrequitable for just one weekend. He was still going to be adored and desired, but the whole situation was going to be only unrequited now, just like your thing for your sister's fine husband.

But I had to get my adoration and desire under control, because he was going to be *right here*, we were going to have conversations, maybe do lunch. And the need burned in me to do something about all that, to make that all come off as smoothly as possible. I burned to be the most amazing American that Jackson Alexander Franklin had ever met. I burned to be perfect in every way to him, just as he was perfect in every way to me.

Mere words cannot express the effect that the thought of this man had on me. They say that some people become hopelessly addicted from just one hit of crack cocaine. I'd often thought that such a thing couldn't be accurate - it had to be an exaggeration. Addiction (as well as its opposite, contempt) only comes with familiarity. *We begin by coveting what we see every day.*

But I was mistaken. I now know that it's quite entirely possible to become addicted to something instantaneously.

I'd been walking around in a constant, heightened state of arousal ever since Episode Four of *The Beekeeper*. Nothing like this level had ever been achieved before, with anyone, real or imagined. He was like a drug to me, a visual, thought-specific aphrodisiac.

And this extra yummy feeling had now climbed into the ionosphere. I'd gone from an initial viewing of an exquisite looking actor playing a character in a make-believe television show, had gone *immediately* to: *I'm gonna meet this guy.* There's no way to fight what something like that does to you. Who would want to fight it?

One subset of the plots involved having the happy couple over to my house after the initial dinner with boring Charlie. I vowed to make them *my* friends, not just *his* relatives.

Although, I reflected, that might be an easier task to accomplish if there was some kind of deeper bond between Charlie and me. You ask me, was I willing to pay some court to boring Charlie to get close to his brother-in-law? Was I willing to date him, become his girlfriend, perhaps even stoop to sleeping with him if necessary?

You bet your sweet ass I was. Friends not fans; this was an opportunity not to be passed up. I would do anything, certainly something so momentary as to entertain Charlie. I would entertain Satan himself to become friends with Jackson Alexander Franklin.

And Charlie was already halfway in love with me anyway. He had been so for years. He couldn't hide it, wasn't even savvy enough to try to hide it, not even smart enough to *want* to try to hide it. There'd be no problem with anything that I might need from Charlie - he was in my hip pocket.

But back to my list. *Get house painted?* I crossed that one off. Let us not be that ridiculous. At least not yet.

The place was a big ol' Craftsman that had belonged to my grandparents, my mom's mom and dad. My grands passed while I was in high school, and Mom rented the place out then. We had our own house, she said, the house that my father had bought for them when they were first married, the house he'd worked all his life to pay for, full of all the memories of her adult life.

Yet when I graduated from college and started working at the firm, in a great gesture, Mom presented the grands' place to me, totally out of the blue. The deed all signed over in my name and everything. It was such a wonderful surprise. My mom was wonderful. I miss her every day.

Like I say, it was a big ol' rambling Craftsman, with hardwood floors and high ceilings, on a long lot, with three bedrooms but only one bathroom. I'd long ago come to believe that indoor plumbing must've been looked upon as some kind of fad in 1909, because why else would they build a huge three bedroom house with only one tiny bathroom? It was an architectural embarrassment. And there was really no place to add another one. Another bathroom would've seemed artificial and added on, like a long barrel on a Tommy gun. Just a glaring mistake.

So it wasn't like they could stay with me in what amounted to a wood and plaster re-enactment of turn of the century privation. Oh, my God, where had that thought come from?

Sometimes my brain ran to more complicated machinations before my mind could catch up to it. No, they couldn't stay with me, even if I had three bathrooms.

I pictured how it would be. Them in one room – I'd have to give them my big bedroom, upstairs. I would stay in the smaller one, downstairs, but not the one directly beneath. The lathe and plaster muffled sound considerably better than drywall; but the floors creaked. So I wouldn't really be able to hear them. I would only be able to *imagine* that I could hear them, the loving couple. I would lay there in my cold bed and imagine that I could hear them, imagine what they were doing. Jackson Alexander Franklin in my house, scant yards away, making love to his beautiful wife. I would never get a minute's sleep. No. They couldn't stay at my house.

But they could definitely visit. And the old place had one definite advantage over Charlie's accommodations - he lived in a high rise condo with all the luxuries, a pool, a gym. I did know that much about him. I remembered when he bought the place, even though I'd somehow been unable to attend the housewarming party.

I didn't have a pool, but I had something infinitely better - I had an enormous backyard, complete with Grandma's extensive garden.

Oh, yeah, it was awesome; Grandma's garden had been her pride and joy. There were raised beds and an arch, with a brick patio with a quaint little fountain in the middle. There were three orange trees and a couple of grapefruit and lemon trees, and cobblestone paths and patches of flowers. There was even the inevitable little potting shed. I remember playing in it when I was a kid, pretending that I was a princess and that it was my castle, in which I waited for Prince Charming to come and sweep me away.

The problem with all this was that Grandma had been gone now for many years, and no gardener was I. The entire backyard was grown over; the morning glories that had been planted on the back fence to lend privacy and seclusion had run absolutely crazy. Like kudzu, they'd grown completely unchecked throughout the whole thing. And everything that wasn't overgrown was dead or dying from lack of irrigation, lack of cultivation, lack of love.

Now that Prince Charming was really, actually coming, I was going to have to do something about that garden, like yesterday. I couldn't let him know that this American princess (who wanted to talk about bees with him) didn't have a garden. Or worse, had an awesome garden, but had let it go to seed. That just wouldn't gibe with the persona that I intended to create for him.

So, on my list, next to *get bees*, I wrote, *find landscaper, fix garden*. Where to begin, though? I didn't know anything about any of this. I picked up the phone and called Uncle Pete.

Uncle Pete was my dad's brother. He and Aunt Polly (yes, I really had an Aunt Polly) owned a little farm outside of town. At least, I'd always thought of it as a farm. They had an orange grove and another big plot under cultivation, planted with vegetables. They had a stand next to the road from which they sold the fruits of their labor. (How clever am I? *Fruits of their labor.* Ha!)

And then there were the bees. I remembered the neat rows of hives, the shed where the honey was extracted and processed, the gleaming metal of the equipment. I remembered seeing Uncle Pete in his beekeepering get up, looking all alien in his big gloves and veiled hat. I remembered the taste of the honey, thick and impossibly, cloyingly sweet on my tongue.

They also sold jars of honey from the fruit stand. I had one of them in my kitchen, although I didn't use it very often. Not much of a cook am I, either. But honey doesn't go bad. That was one fact I knew already.

SIXTEEN

Uncle Pete was glad to see me, and Aunt Polly kissed my forehead and told me that I'd grown into a beautiful woman. She told me this every time she saw me. She ran into the house to make lunch, and Uncle Pete and I walked out to where the hives were.

"So, you want some bees?" he said, cocking his head curiously at me. The gesture touched my heart - it reminded me so much of my dad.

"Have you ever heard of Jake Franklin, Uncle Pete? *The Face of Canadian Beekeeping*?"

Uncle Pete looked at me, frowned. "Am I a Canadian beekeeper? We got our own problems right here, kiddo," he said, a shade of annoyance in his voice.

I would notice that these bee people would become annoyed with any questions of a philosophical nature about bees. They were facing their own troubles, their own devastating losses, and discussions of the thoughts and theories of their brethren in far flung locales just irritated them. Something had to be done here, first, and everywhere else could wait. I thought then as I would all along, that maybe if they could all get together and reach come kind of consensus, if they could all try to tackle this tragedy together, maybe they could get somewhere.

But I had Uncle Pete's number, I had a plan, and I wasn't concerned with his beekeeper's problems at that point. Maybe I would listen to them later, so I would have something to talk to Jake about, but right now, I had to set up the illusion of my own hobby.

Anybody remember *Bewitched*? Samantha was a witch and all that, but more importantly for my plans, Darren was an adman. Many episodes revolved around him and Larry and Samantha hopelessly entrenched in some situation or other where they had to impress a client, usually by pretending to somehow be into whatever outlandish habits the client was into. With the sprinkling of a little witchcraft into the mix, hilarity ensued.

So I laid it all out for Uncle Pete, just like an episode of *Bewitched*.

"Jake Franklin is a Canadian actor, Uncle Pete. He was in a show called *The Beekeeper* about ten years ago."

"Never heard of it," Uncle Pete replied, just like I knew he would.

"Yeah, no, you wouldn't have. It only played in Canada. Anyway, this guy is also a big activist for bees up there. I guess he has appeared before their parliament or whatever it is they have, talking about the Colony Collapse Disorder and all that, demanding that the government do something, et cetera."

"So?"

"Well, like I say, he's an actor. He has retained the firm to represent him in contract negotiations for some movie he's doing here in the States. He and his wife are actually going to relocate here while he's making this movie.

"There are a lot of contract lawyers around, Uncle Pete. So, I've been tapped to make Mr. Franklin's stay as comfortable as possible. As interesting as possible. If he's not bored, if he's entertained, the idea of perhaps retaining a cheaper or more experienced law firm will not occur to him. Do you see where this is going?"

Uncle Pete smiled, and again I was reminded of Dad.

"So, I need your help. You remember my grandma and grandpa's house? The one with the garden?"

"Yeah, we all had Christmas there a couple of times, when you were a little girl."

I smiled. "Well, I live there now. The plan is to get the garden going again, bring in some bees, have the Canadian and his wife over for a visit, let them see that we're also beekeepers here in the States, make them feel at home. Show them a little loyalty, guarantee that they won't go law firm shopping should contract negotiations turn out not to be everything they'd hoped." I paused, then added, "And of course, any advice and equipment that you might furnish, well, that would all be generously compensated for by the firm."

This was a lie, of course. The firm didn't operate like a 1960's sitcom. Uncle Pete would indeed be compensated; money was hardly an object in the endeavor of making my dreams come true. But the compensation would come right out of my savings account.

I could tell from Uncle Pete's smile that he bought the whole thing, hook, line and sinker. Life would be so much better if the plots were like sitcoms, and Uncle Pete believed it could be so.

SEVENTEEN

So the garden renovation began. Uncle Pete and his cronies, his various farmer and landscaper minions, installed a horticultural renaissance that rivaled anything on *Home Makeover: Extreme Edition*. It wasn't cheap, but I was amazed that after only a short week, the backyard was transformed. All the arrogant morning glories were gone; sod was installed where grass was supposed to be, mature flowers grew in their nooks, vegetables in the garden, something already climbing halfway up the arch. It almost looked like all that stuff had been growing there for years, cared for, tenderly and expertly. They even put in new lighting, got the fountain running again and refurbished the built-in barbeque that stood in one corner.

"I have a guy that'll come out a couple times a month and cut the grass. Just make sure it all stays watered." Uncle Pete sipped an ice tea I'd made especially for him. "Almost everything I had them plant needs bees for pollination. Your Canadian guy will recognize that. You already have the oranges and the lemons; but now you also have onions, and blueberries; that's a cucumber going over the arch. I also fit you in a little avocado tree. No sense planting any apples or cherries, because they need a cold snap. They wouldn't produce much here. For flowers, you got some crocuses, some wild lilac. In the summer you should get some hostas in, for the shady spots, and some snapdragons. For fall, some asters and zinnias."

"And the bees?"

"I figured we should go back to the house, and I'll refresh your memory a little bit, reinforce your beekeeping skills. Then we'll put a couple of hives in the truck and bring them over here. Three should be more than sufficient. And I even have a surprise for you. It should really impress the Canadian."

I gave him a big hug. "I love you, Uncle Pete!" And I really meant it, more than he could ever know. "The firm loves you!"

"Anything for the bees," he replied. "Anything for you and the firm."

The surprise he had in store for me was something called a Top Bar Beehive. He had constructed it for me himself, with his gnarled, scarred farmer's hands, so like Dad's scarred, gnarled mechanic's hands. Unlike a traditional beehive with wooden frames and a beeswax media upon which the bees constructed their combs (which was called a *Langstroth* hive, I would learn from the ever helpful *Wikipedia*), a top bar hive used no media. The bees just built their combs attached to the wooden bars that ran across the top. These hives weren't the square white boxes that we are all familiar with. They're instead tapered, almost triangular in shape.

The honey produced in such a set up couldn't be extracted in the centrifuge, Uncle Pete explained, so the top bar hive wasn't valuable in large scale honey production. But the honey that came out of these was better, he told me with a wink, and the whole thing overall was better for the bees. He said, "They probably don't have too many of these in Canada, because it gets so cold up there. They're best in temperate climates. But I'm sure your boy will have heard of them."

We drove back out to the farm, and Uncle Pete showed me how to do the important beekeeping duties. He commented that I was a quick study, and I thought, *You'd be a quick study too, if you looked at something you were trying to learn as if your life depended on learning it.* And in my mind, my life, my future possible friendship with the godlike *Face of Canadian Beekeeping*, most assuredly depended on my absorbing and assimilating every single detail that Uncle Pete could teach me. And it wasn't really rocket science. After I got over the initial feelings of claustrophobia in the outfit, I found the slow, definite movements of the craft to be oddly therapeutic and calming.

Uncle Pete hooked me up with all the essential equipment. He made sure all the stuff was old and worn "for authenticity," he said. Uncle Pete was completely committed to the charade I'd laid out for him.

"No one will believe that you've been doing this for any length of time if you have all new stuff." He gave me Aunt Polly's old outfit, grinning when he told me that she would be so thrilled to get a new one. All on the firm's dime, or so he thought.

For the next week or so, I spent all my evenings on the internet, studying up on the apian universe. Canadian beekeeping, American beekeeping, Colony Collapse Disorder, mites, viruses, fungi, insecticides, all the warring theories, what was being done, what wasn't being done. The only thing about bees I didn't have any time for was *The Beekeeper*. No time to sigh over pictures, no time to go to the Cathedral of Jackson Alexander Franklin and worship with *CanadaBees*.

After this week of intensive study, I called Uncle Pete and had him quiz me. He pronounced me an expert, vowed that "the Canadian boy," as he oh, so adorably referred to him, would undoubtedly be impressed.

Oh, Uncle Pete! If only you realized how entirely I longed to impress the Canadian boy! With every cell of my being.

Now that the beekeeping arena was conquered, now that I felt confident that Jake and I would be able to converse about it into the wee hours of the morning, now it was time to turn my attention to Charles J. Bakke.

Now it was time to insert myself into his little, boring world. I decided that the best plan would be to have myself introduced to Jake and Shirley as Charlie's new girlfriend. Hell, I still had six weeks left before they were supposed to arrive. By then, I'd make sure that I was his girlfriend indeed, not just his *new* girlfriend.

It really was all too simple, O, my brothers. A piece of cake, a can of corn. On Friday (t-minus 44 days to arrival) I arranged it so that at 11:45, I *just happened* to be standing outside of my office in reception, looking at a file. Out of the corner of my eye, I watched Dan Silver, the other contract lawyer, walk in to Charlie's office to fetch him for lunch.

They walked out and Charlie paused. "Hey," he said, as if the thought had never occurred to him before, "would you like to have lunch with us?"

I narrowed my eyes, glanced at the clock. Unspoken was, *how dare you ask me to lunch fifteen minutes before lunch is scheduled to begin? Seriously, Charlie, you should know better than that.* But I sounded *so* disappointed when I said, "I'm sorry, Charlie. I have plans. Purrrr-haps some other time."

Charlie was shy, but he wasn't stupid. He watched *Mad Men*, and he had Silver standing there to impress. He was shy, but not at all gutless. He never gave up, and no amount of turn-downs seemed to faze him. So he threw it out there again. "How about dinner then?"

Oh, Charlie, if only you knew that I wouldn't turn you down again. If only you knew that I would do anything necessary to bind you to me, just to get close to your scrumptious brother-in-law.

"That sounds great." I lowered my eyelashes shyly, so he wouldn't see me witness the surprise on his face. I gave it a split second, and then looked up at him. "What time?"

The surprise was still there, and he stammered, looked at Silver, looked back at me. "Uh . . . Say, eight o'clock?"

I smiled, wrote my phone number down on a sticky from the receptionist's desk. I walked over to him, ignoring Silver, and handed it to him. "It's a date then."

I left the file on the receptionist's desk, and walked slowly away, toward the elevators, towards my mythical lunch date. I knew I looked like a million bucks, especially to Charlie. I heard Silver whisper, "Hot damn, Bakke! I told you that she couldn't keep saying no forever."

I smiled to myself as I got on the elevator. No more no's, Charlie. You lucky dog. You unsuspecting, entirely necessary, infinitely useful, lucky, lucky dog.

EIGHTEEN

In the six weeks that followed, my plan for Charlie's seduction came off like clockwork. When I got back from lunch that Friday, I wrote down the sequence, and then proceeded to follow my own play book, event by event, milestone by milestone. First date, first kiss, first heavy petting, first denial - "What kind of a girl do you think I am, Charlie? You don't have any respect for me!"

First promise of respect, first protestation of love. First surrender. The decision to treat it all, if not as an out-and-out secret, at least to keep it on the down-low at work. Of course, everyone that cared would know, but no official words, no PDA's would be permitted.

The morning that Charlie announced that he would be picking up his sister and brother-in-law at the airport that evening, he believed us to be soul mates. I even suspected that an engagement ring might be in the offing.

Charlie said that they would get all settled in and catch-up that night, and Jake would be coming in the following morning to begin discussing his contract. "We can all have lunch together," he suggested. "Talk about bees."

That night, ritualistically, I rid myself of the mountain of evidence proving my obsession with, my worship of, Jackson Alexander Franklin. All You-Tube videos of his interviews were deleted from my laptop. The five favorite pictures of him that I kept in the gallery on my phone - deleted. *The Beekeeper* poster deleted as the background on my desktop. *CanadaBees'* blog and all the other fan sites deleted from my favorites list. *The Beekeeper* television series gone from my *Netflix* queue.

I'd hesitated however, when I went to do away with all of his pictures. *Bear with me,* I thought. *My heart is in the electronic coffin there with those pictures, and I must pause till it come back to me.*

I'd spent a lot of loving hours collecting all those images of the dear visage. I'd spent so many more hours achingly watching them go by on the screen saver. In the end, I couldn't just delete them, send them to oblivion. Instead, I burned them to a disk and threw it into the back of my desk drawer, unlabeled. Then I deleted them all from the hard drive.

NINETEEN

I dressed to the teeth on the day that Jackson Alexander Franklin was scheduled to appear at my firm. But nothing overtly sexy. Just fine, conservative, expensive business attire, my most awesome heels, my most flawless make-up.

Let me explain the layout of the office for you. A bank of floor to ceiling glass windows faced the elevators, so when someone got off they could be observed walking up the hall before entering through the glass door. A receptionist's desk was in the middle of the room; a couch and coffee table was to the right of her desk, where the clients could wait until their lawyer showed up. My office, also walled on one side with glass, was directly behind and a little to the right of the reception area, against the back wall. Charlie's office (the corner one) was to the right of mine. A file room was to my left.

A surreptitious glance at Charlie's calendar had let me know that Prince Charming was due to arrive at 9 am. I sat at my desk, absent-mindedly shuffling files around, trying to look busy. I should've been busy, there was a ton of work to be done, but it was the farthest thing from my mind. Work? What the fuck was that? I was going to meet Jackson Alexander Franklin today! I still couldn't entirely believe that it was going to happen.

At 8:42, one of the elevators dinged. It was a sound I'd long ago ceased to notice. If you listened to the elevators ding all day long, you'd go crazy; so the sound had long ago been relegated to white background noise in my perception. But not today. I had looked up at every elevator ding since 7:30 that morning.

It all happened in slow motion. Jake stepped out of the elevator. He was wearing a perfectly tailored, very expensive, dark blue pinstriped suit, a shirt as white as virgin Canada snow and a powder blue tie, and a pair of Ray-Bans. I thought, not for the first time, that the man should always wear blue.

I realized that I'd stopped breathing, and forced myself to start again.

Jake paused, and next, brother Greg stepped off the elevator. He wore a black suit, a little less conservative than Jake's, but of the same flawless cut. He wore the same white white shirt and an emerald green tie. To my surprise and delight, no wifey was in evidence.

They walked up the hall toward the door, again in slow motion, or so it seemed to me. No one noticed them, these two exquisite looking, perfectly turned-out men. There was no cadre of fan girls laying in wait to mob *The Beekeeper* for an autograph. This was America, after all, where he was completely unknown. One of my new paralegals, Linda Somebody, was walking in the opposite direction and she did look up from the brief she was reading as they passed by. She didn't stop, but did look over her shoulder. I made a mental note that it was high time for Miss Linda to be assigned some research in the firm's file vault. In the basement.

I watched them speak to Maria, the receptionist. If Maria was impressed, she didn't let it show. That was what I liked best about Maria. She was a professional. Jake and Greg stood there talking, waiting for Charlie to come up to get them.

I reflected that we'd had a few minor actors as clients before, and they always showed up in casual clothes, sometimes even sweats. To American actors, even minor ones, it wasn't necessary to impress lawyers; lawyers were employees.

But not my Canadian boys. These negotiations were important, maybe direction-changing for Jake's career. He and his brother didn't regard this firm only as an expensive employee. We were the people that were going to help them to conquer Hollywood.

Charlie finally showed up. I watched Jake clap him on the shoulder, shake his hand. I watched Jake introduce (or possibly re-introduce) his brother-in-law to his brother, his manager. And then the three of them started walking toward my office. Again it all seemed to be in slow motion, each stride reverberating in my heart. Jake and Charlie were in animated conversation, and didn't look in my direction as they passed. I thought that I might have to punish Charlie for that.

Greg walked a pace behind them, and he looked in my direction and smiled right at me as he passed. *By the pricking of my thumbs, something wicked this way comes.* I smiled back and lowered my lashes at the frank appraisal in his eyes. When I looked up again, all three of them were gone.

Their meeting lasted exactly 47 minutes. I know, because I felt every tick of the clock. When they at last emerged from Charlie's office, I was on the phone, and he nodded at me and paused outside my open door, talking with his new clients, his relatives, waiting for me to get off the phone.

Fortunately, I was talking to Uncle Pete, and told him I had to go. I listened to the phone go dead, listened to the dial tone, all so that I could just look at Jackson Alexander Franklin for a minute, and try to get my breathing in order.

I knew that he was thirty-eight now, and the years since *The Beekeeper* looked great on him. The full, perfect mouth had firmed up a little bit; there were barely perceptible laugh lines on his face, a few crows-feet around the exquisite eyes. His hair was still as black as coal, not a gray hair to be seen. He didn't look a day over twenty-eight or so, and I again wondered what they had in the water up there, that everybody looked ten years younger than they actually were. He was, if anything, more flawless than I could've imagined, and when I discovered that I wasn't breathing again, I took a deep breath and hung up the phone.

It was then that I noticed that his manager had been watching me. When I hung up, he tapped his brother on the shoulder. Jake stopped talking to Charlie, and the three of them entered my office.

Like I've said, I'm not shy, and I've never been afraid to meet anyone. And since first impressions are so very important, I'd steeled myself for *this* meeting, had practiced in front of the mirror, had thought up half a dozen clever things to say, if the need arose. There would be no stammering, no losing my voice, no forgetting my name. This introduction was far too important to screw up with some adolescent lack of control.

With all the grace I possessed, I arose and came around from behind my desk as they entered. Charlie spoke first. "Greg Franklin, this is my . . . My *colleague*, Marina Phillips."

Greg smiled that same appraising, killer smile and shook my hand. His grasp was firm and he hung on to my hand just a split second more than was either customary or polite, his eyes never leaving mine. "*So* nice to meet you," he said, finally releasing my hand.

And then the moment arrived. The moment for which I'd waited a lifetime. He stuck out his hand and said, "Hi, I'm Jake Franklin. But you can call me Zander. Everyone does."

Everyone most assuredly does not, I thought, *or I would've heard about it from CanadaBees*. I slowly, carefully took the outstretched hand in mine and he shook it, then released it immediately, as befitted someone who shook hands for a living.

"I understand we're having dinner tonight," quoth he.

His voice, his words struck my poor brain and registered as if he was intimating that he and I were having dinner tonight, together, *alone*, just the two of us.

He hadn't meant this at all, of course, and not for the last time, when I'd speak to Jackson Alex - no, wait, *Zander*, was it? Not for the last time, when I'd discourse with *Zander* Franklin, I would get the impression that I might be losing my mind.

But I was cool, my pedigree chums. I was so cool, ice cubes wouldn't melt in my pockets. I smiled at him, this object of my deepest, darkest, wettest fantasies, and said simply, "That's the plan."

To avoid staring at him (did I not say I was cool?), I looked at Greg, only to discover that he was rather staring at me. I said, "Will you be joining us too, Mr. Franklin?"

His eyebrows went up at the *Mr. Franklin*. "Please, call me Greg." He looked at his brother and brother-in-law (I realized all at once that he was Charlie's brother-in-law, too) as if for confirmation.

Charlie said, "Ah, yeah, sure, Greg. You know you're always welcome."

Greg looked at me, as did Jake - no, it was *Zander*. He smiled that adorable, just slightly crooked smile, so incredibly much more adorable in person and said, "'Till then, then."

I nodded, they nodded, and Charlie seamlessly ushered them out of my office. I watched him escort them out into the hall, watched him stand there in front of the elevators with them. He and Zander were talking about something funny, both of them rocking back on their heels in glee. I imagined it was some shared remembrance, some inside joke, perhaps. When I looked at Greg, I found that he was looking at me. He smiled, and again I smiled and lowered my lashes. When I looked up again, they were gone.

I guessed that Charlie had forgotten all about the four of us doing lunch; after all, it was only 10 o'clock in the morning. But I thought he might need to be punished for this, too.

When he came back up, Charlie informed me that they weren't staying with him after all, at least not yet, because Greg had booked them into a hotel. He smiled at me, that doofy look that was supposed to secretly reference our on-the-down-low love affair. I smiled back.

"I've got a million things to do," he said. "I'll see you tonight."

TWENTY

I arrived at his house at seven, dinner being scheduled for eight. I had Charlie so well trained that he wouldn't even have dreamt of suggesting any sort of intimate romp before his guests arrived. He knew better. Such activities would smear my make-up.

God love Charlie, though. He was a feminist through and through, even though I don't think he realized it. He didn't cook, and he didn't naturally assume that I did either. So he'd shamelessly had the dinner catered, from the finest restaurant in town, delivered and set up. A huge peasant meal, consisting of an array of deceptively simple Italian courses.

I had dressed plainly, yet elegantly, of course. Casual, but not sexy. I was waiting to take my lead from Sharon, or whatever her name was. Waiting to see how my Canadian boys liked their women to dress.

At 8:15 they arrived, not even fashionably late by any means.

Now came my first opportunity to meet his wife, *the most fortunate woman in Canada. In the world*, I thought; *no sense just confining it to Canada. She was the most fortunate woman in the world.*

She hugged her brother then smiled eagerly at me while he introduced me, then just threw all convention to the wind and went right ahead and hugged me, too. "It's so nice to finally meet you!" she said in complete sincerity. "I've heard so much about you!"

I mentally patted myself on the back at that one, could almost picture that engagement ring. Charlie had told his sister about me. Wasn't that sweet? "Nice to meet you, too!"

She grabbed me by the hand and led me a little away from the men. "We have so much to talk about! I have so many things to tell you about Charlie!" she threatened. "He's such a goof! But I'm sure you already know that!"

Yeah, I know Charlie's a goof, all right, I thought. But probably not in the way she meant.

He looked a trifle nervous and said, "Yeah, all that can wait. Let's eat."

Charlie pulled out my chair and seated me at the foot of the table, then seated himself at its head. The fortunate Mrs. Franklin sat to my right, with her husband to her right. Brother Greg was seated to my left.

I mostly observed during the excellent Italian dinner. I had taken half a Valium before arriving (I had my own prescription now), just to keep my nerves in check, and what with the wine, I grew mellow indeed. I looked at them, joined in the conversation where appropriate, the very air around my head choked with Canadian accents, all those strangely distorted short vowels.

I noticed with no little curiosity that while his brother called him *Zander*, Charlie and his own wife called him *Jake*. How strange and wonderful it seemed to me that he would ask me to call him *Zander*.

She wore blue; she would probably always wear blue. It was a simple but expensive frock, and it fitted her perfectly (I thought that they had excellent tailors in Canada, along with their excellent water). It was low cut, yet still demure and the hue and fabric brought out the perfection of her peaches and cream complexion, the glow of her turquoise eyes, the glint of her blonde hair, done up in a delightful Gibson girl style.

While we ate, while we talked, I couldn't help but notice how often she touched him, on the shoulder, on the wrist. And I couldn't help but notice either how much he touched her back, on her bare arm, on her hand. They made for an adorable couple, and if I haven't mentioned it before, I must repeat at this juncture that I hated her utterly.

Charlie said, "Sheila!" once, and I wondered who the hell he was talking to. Then I realized that was her name. *Sheila.* I'd started to identify her simply as *Mrs. Franklin* in my mind, because I was having so much trouble remembering her name. *She's the luckiest bitch in the world,* I thought, *why can I not remember her name?*

Maybe looking at all those pictures of her husband had left a lesion on my brain, a lesion that had obliterated the gray matter assigned to remembering the name of the wife of the most desirable man in the world. I smiled at my own humor, but nobody noticed. I conjured up a map of Australia in my mind, to use as a mnemonic. They called their women *sheilas* in Australia, did they not? I thought that this might help me to remember her name.

The Canadian boys were dressed casually, but to the nines. Once glance and you could tell that they were both clothes horses, and the race was a dead heat. I timed my gaze at Prince Charming, made it just long enough to look interested in what he was saying, but not long enough to be staring. When I looked at Greg, again, he was already looking at me.

When the meal concluded, dutifully, I helped Sharon, Shelly, *Sheila* clear away the dinner dishes, as if I was as devoted a wifey as she was. In the kitchen, she again grabbed my hand and said, "I'm so happy to meet Charlie's girlfriend! It'll be so nice to have a friend in the States, someone I can talk to while we're here! We can go shopping!"

I thought I'd like nothing better than to paint a bull's-eye on her forehead and go shopping for ammo, but I said enthusiastically, "Oh, yeah! That'll be great!"

Charlie came into the kitchen and kissed me possessively on the cheek. "More wine," he said, grabbed another bottle and the corkscrew, and the three of us joined the Canadian boys once again.

The next thing that I noticed was that these were some drinkers, these Canadians. I had to closely monitor my own intake, as I was already half in the bag due to my somewhat recreational use of the Valium earlier. And they smoked, these Canadian men, except for Charlie.

I was intrigued and pleasantly surprised at this little vice. I remembered a scene from Season Two, where the beekeeper chastises the lady cop for smoking around the hives, telling her that "nicotine is an insecticide." She was suitably chagrined, seeing that this faux pas had dropped her another rung, pushed her another step back from the never to be achieved pinnacle of his affection. I had felt deeply for her.

I had a pack of Kools in my desk at home, and would indulge in one on occasion. It was a grievous fault, however, and grievously had I always answered it. My mother would've slapped me in the mouth if she'd ever caught me smoking. It was just not ladylike, not businesslike in her eyes.

"Can I trouble you for one of those?" I asked Greg as he went to light another cigarette off of the one he was about to put out. Charlie looked at me in surprise, but fuck him, he wasn't my mother.

"They're Canadian," Greg warned. He handed me the green pack, foreign, long and flat, with the name *Dunhill* on it.

"Then it'll be something different," I said, shaking one of them out. I didn't mean for it to sound like I was flirting with him, but that was exactly how it sounded. Fortunately, the others were having a conversation over our heads and didn't notice.

I put the cigarette to my lips and he lit it, smiling at me all the while. I looked away, looked at the weird package for a moment. They were menthols; my own poison of choice. I went to give it back to him, but he held up his hand.

"Keep it," he said, "in the spirit of international . . . relations. I have another pack."

"How nice of you," I said sincerely, thinking that he would be hard pressed to find another pack of Canadian coffin nails in this town when the ones he had ran out. I made a mental note to buy him some real cigarettes, some American cigarettes, the next time I passed by a smoke shop. But I didn't look at him again. His smile was dangerous.

We all got slowly, cheerfully, inevitably drunk. I felt myself to be a little ahead of them, actually, what with the mother's little helper and all. We talked about trivialities, current world events. A couple times they got off on Canadian tangents, but after a moment, they always politely brought the conversation back to topics that I could ken.

When the third bottle of wine was dead, I volunteered to go out to the kitchen and get the next one. I picked up the corkscrew from the table and somewhat unsteadily weaved to the kitchen. Once there, for some unknown, drunken reason, I decided to attempt to open it myself. I augured the corkscrew into the cork and was gamely trying to pull it out, when I heard Greg's voice and looked up to see him standing there.

"Please," he said. "Allow me."

Swiftly, before I could react, he came around behind me and pressed his body against mine, covering both my hands on the corkscrew and the wine bottle with his own. He exerted pressure against my hands, against my body, slowly working the corkscrew back and forth.

My body, so completely worked up from my reaction to Zander's presence, not only didn't object to this untoward familiarity, but melted back into his, quite of its own volition. He held me tightly, laid his cheek against mine, and worked the corkscrew slowly back and forth for what seemed like an eternity.

At last the cork popped, and he deftly put his thumb over the opening, taking the bottle from my hands and releasing me, all in one smooth motion. He faced me and took a swig from it, never taking his eyes from mine.

He handed the bottle to me, and for something to do, I took a swig myself. Still, he held my gaze.

Then he leaned in and whispered in my ear. "I must say that I'm very flattered, Marina. But what kind of homewrecker would I be if I just swooped in here from the Great White North and seduced my brother-in-law's ever so lovely girlfriend? How would the contract negotiations fall out then?"

He moved back to see my reaction. I opened my mouth to object, but he put a finger to my lips. "But I think that we're going to be great friends. Yeah. We're going to be great friends."

He took the bottle from me and headed for the kitchen door. At that moment, the door swung open and Zander came in, *Zander*, the true cause of all my warm feelings. He smiled at us innocently, that incredible smile, and I was sure that I couldn't possibly do anything else but die right then, die from my completely unrequited, completely unrequitable love for him, just drop dead right there in Charlie's kitchen. Greg handed him the bottle and clapped him around the shoulder, and they left the kitchen. I didn't die, but followed them back out into the dining room.

The rest of the evening passed uneventfully. Greg mostly didn't look at me anymore, except for the occasions that he smiled at me.

We killed the fourth bottle of wine, and it was at last time for them to go back to the hotel. Mrs. Franklin gave me a big hug, and repeated again how glad she was to meet me. I stood stock still while Jackson Alexander Franklin took me in his strong, perfect arms and gave me a brief, entirely brotherly hug. I didn't trust myself to hug him back. Then brother Greg kissed me lightly on the cheek, and said, "*So* nice to meet you."

Charlie went downstairs and poured them into a cab. I couldn't even face the entirely depressing thought of taking out my lust for Zander on him, and when he returned, I was already passed out, immersed in a deep, dreamless sleep.

It wasn't until the next day that I realized that the subject of bees had not come up once.

TWENTY-ONE

The next morning I was at my desk, bright and early as usual, because I, too, am nothing if not a professional. I would gamely combat my hangover, fulfill my duties. There was a ton of work to do. Charlie had wheeshed out and called in sick.

I'd just swallowed two more aspirins and was rubbing my temples when the phone rang. I picked it up: it was Maria, the receptionist. "There's a Mr. Franklin here to see you."

My heart stopped and I looked up. Greg was standing there in reception, looking at me, a watchful smirk on his face. I willed my expression to not show any disappointment. Instead, I smiled brightly and said into the phone, "Send him in."

I watched him smile, nod, thank Maria. I watched him stride across the short distance to my office, watched him as he entered, shut the door, took a chair in front of my desk. All the while, I wondered what *the hell* this was going to be about.

"Hey, Marina," he said. "How are you?"

"I'm a little hung over," I admitted. "Does everyone in Canada drink like you people?"

He grinned. "We start young - drinking age in Canada is nineteen. Wait 'til we bust out the Bloody Caesars - it's a Canadian Bloody Mary. With Clamato. And horseradish. Best cure for a hangover."

My queasy stomach tried to turn over at the thought of that one. "What can I do for you?"

"I was supposed to pick up some paperwork from Charlie, but the receptionist said he didn't make it in today. I figure he's getting soft, been away from home too long."

"Yeah, I don't think Charlie is too much of a drinker."

He grinned innocently. "You don't know?"

I didn't reply, annoyed at being caught out in my non-familiarity with my supposed boyfriend's habits.

Greg grinned again. "Yeah, I was wondering about all that. How did you and Charlie get together, anyway? He seems a little sedate for you. I wouldn't peg you guys as compatible. He just doesn't seem to be your type. To make Charlie seem interesting, you must need quite the imagination."

My eyebrows went up in surprise at this dead-on observation, this insult to my supposed boyfriend. But I said nothing.

When it became clear that I wasn't going to qualify all this speculation with an answer, Greg shrugged. "Anyway, since it looks like no business is going to be transacted today, I was wondering, can you get out of here? The happy couple is either still asleep or out sight-seeing, your boyfriend is down for the count, and I'm at odds and ends. You're the only other person I know in this town. Can you get out of here? I'll buy you brunch."

When I hesitated, he said, "Look, I want to apologize about last night. When I get a little loaded, sometimes I get a little frisky in the presence of beautiful women. I didn't mean anything by it. I'm really not that way at all." When I hesitated still, he said it again. "Really, I'm not that way at all. I'm sorry." He stuck out his hand, smiled winningly. "Friends?"

I shook his hand and smiled. "Friends."

"Great! Let's get out of here."

How could I refuse? Here was Zander's brother, asking to be my friend. This was a much, much better in than poor ol' boring Charlie. Charlie was only *her* brother, and it has already been established how much I despised *her*. Greg was *his* brother, and he was good-looking and sexy and charming and dangerous to boot, and he was asking to be friends. Oh, yeah, this was a much better in.

I told Maria that I would be handling Mr. Bakke's meeting for him, and walked out to the elevators with Greg.

TWENTY-TWO

I started toward my car in the parking lot, but he stopped me. "Let's walk," he said. "I know a place."

We walked the short distance to *Paul's*, one of the best restaurants in town. Greg strode in as if we owned the place, and as we approached the maître d', the man said, "Ah, Mr. Franklin! So nice to see you this morning! How are you?"

I was impressed. Only in town a couple of days, and the maître d' at *Paul's* called him by name. I'd been in the place probably ten times in the last two months. The maître d' didn't call me by name.

"A little rough, Sammy, I must say."

"I'm sorry to hear that, Mr. Franklin. How can I help?"

"How about a couple of those drinks I showed you how to make?"

The maître d' smiled. "Right this way, sir."

"Who says Americans aren't polite?" Greg was smooth, but I wasn't too hung over to not notice the green flash of the $50 as it passed from Canadian to American when they shook hands. "Bring four to start off with."

Sammy showed us to a dim back booth, a perfect spot for nursing a hangover. Moments later, I was stirring a vile-looking tomato juice and God-only knew what else concoction with a celery stick.

Greg put a spoonful of horseradish into his, stirred it and drank half of it in one gulp. He took a bite of his celery stick, and then said, "So, tell me more about you and Charlie." Again I just looked at him. "Rather not go there? Ok. Tell me about your imagination, then."

"Why do you keep bringing that up?"

"Oh, I don't know. You just strike me as a girl with big dreams."

"Doesn't everyone have big dreams?"

"Some have bigger dreams than others. More specific, *more planned-out* big dreams."

I sipped my drink. It was just as awful as it looked, spicy and burning. I'd never become a fan of Bloody Caesars, that was for sure.

I didn't like the drift of this conversation, either, didn't like the way Greg Franklin seemed to be able to read my mind. If he thought I was going to make some big confession to him, he was sadly mistaken. *Sore-y*, my pedigree Canadian chum.

"My dreams aren't any bigger or any more planned out than anyone else's," I replied firmly. He took another chomp from his celery stick, nodded, and drained off the rest of his evil drink. "What about you?" I asked. "What's your story?"

He grinned, that devilish, shark's smile, showing all his teeth. "Oh, baby, I am living my dream." When this declaration failed to elicit a response from me, he continued. "My story? Let's see. I was born in Canada, but I mostly grew up in a little town in Michigan. Adrian."

"I thought you grew up on some kind of farm in Canada."

The shark's grin again. "No. *Zander* grew up on some kind of farm in Canada."

Damned if he hadn't caught me again. But I wasn't daunted. "Aren't you brothers? I just naturally assumed that brothers grow up together."

"We're *step-brothers*, Marina. My father met Zander's mother on a trip up North. The first time I met him was at their wedding. It was a spring wedding, and he'd just turned sixteen. I was twenty."

He paused, and I kept right on looking at him, even though the idea of a sixteen-year-old Zander Franklin slid effortlessly through my mind.

He said, "I was in Chicago at the time, trying to break into the music business. Not succeeding."

I figured that he probably wanted me to ask him about that, but I was too caught up in this new revelation. Jackson Alexander Franklin had once been an only child, just like me.

Obviously, Franklin Senior, Greg's father, had legally adopted him at some point, or his last name wouldn't be Franklin. I wondered what *CanadaBees* would do with all this insider information. Completely intrigued now, I waited for him to continue.

"So when Dad called and told me that he was going to get married, I took all the money I had left and flew up North to see what was up. Always one to make an entrance, I just showed up, didn't tell Dad I was coming. He was *so* glad to see me.

"The first time I saw Zander was there at the wedding He was wearing a rented tux, and I could tell it must've been his first time in big-boy clothes, caused he looked as uncomfortable as hell."

Greg paused again, and I got the unsettling impression that he did so just so I could once again picture sixteen-year-old Zander, this time in a tuxedo.

Greg continued. "The bride was lovely. I didn't see much of a family resemblance between her and Zander, but she does have the same black hair. Not much to tell after that. Dad was glad to see me, and the new wife (who insisted that I call her Mom) was overjoyed to meet me. Zander was thrilled at the prospect of suddenly having an older brother.

"There was nothing to draw me back to Chicago, so I took them up on their gracious offer to stay with them. I worked on the farm with them. Went to school."

For something to say, I asked, "What are Canadian parents like, anyway?"

He tilted his head at the odd question, tossed off half of his second drink, took another bite of celery, chewed, ruminated. "Dad was just Dad. My own mother had passed when I was nine. That's why we moved to Michigan. Dad wanted to get away from the memories."

He paused again, and I took another sip from my drink. It was still awful.

Greg continued. "So, yeah, I guess I did have a Canadian Mom, even if it was kinda late. She was strict. We had to be home by 7 on school nights, 9:30 on weekends, by her decree. I was twenty, for Christ's sake, and I could've rebelled. But she'd taken me in, out of the goodness of her heart, and I loved it there. It was really not too much to ask, anyway. It wasn't like there was a whole lot of night life going on. The prohibitions were for Zander's sake, really. Zander is the spitting image of his dad: same blue eyes, same crooked smile."

Again he paused, and again I pictured a teenaged Zander.

"His dad was also called Jake – his name was *Jackson Robert*. So Mom called her son *Zander* for *Jackson Alexander*. No one else calls him that but Mom and me." He squinted curiously at me again. "*And now you.*" I raised my eyebrows noncommittally at him, and he continued. "I guess the story goes that ol' Jackson Robert was quite the charmer, and a little bit of a drinker. He spent a lot of time at the local bar of an evening, after the crop was in. This was a common practice, I guess. Once upon a time, if men wanted to ignore their families, they had to get out of the house to do it. No sitting in front of the computer playing video games. They had to get out, go to the lodge or the bar. I never heard any stories that he cheated on Mom or anything like that, but still, I guess he was legendary for his way with the ladies.

"One night, I guess Jackson Robert was paying a little too much attention to one of the bar flies at the local tavern. Her ol' man took exception to it. An altercation ensued, and the guy shot him dead in the parking lot."

I choked on my drink, started to cough uncontrollably. Greg signaled to a waiter and got me a glass of water. I gulped it gratefully and pushed the Caesar aside.

When I stopped coughing, Greg continued. "I guess Zander was about twelve years old at the time. But it didn't take too many years before it became obvious to Mom that he was going to grow up to be just as much of a charmer as her husband had ever been. So she took the situation in hand. The farm girls that he went to high school with had already discovered him, had already started calling the house looking for him by the time I moved in.

"I remember one little girl, her name was Sarah. Zander had made the innocent mistake of asking her to help him with his math homework, and she started calling the house right after school. He wasn't home and she called like nine times before he finally breezed in.

"I can still hear Mom yelling at him. 'You cannot just give out your phone number to these young ladies, Zander! I haven't had a moment's peace all afternoon!'

"And then, softer, 'You simply cannot take advantage of these girls, Zander, just because you can. *Just because they'll let you*. It isn't *right*. Young girls, girls in general, sometimes they're a little crazy. Never forget what happened to your father.'

"'Okay, Mom,' he said. 'I won't.'

"I remember him coming out on the back porch, where I was sitting on the steps, smoking a cigarette. He had a thoughtful, *What just happened?* kind of look on his face. I glanced up at him and said, 'Woman troubles, kid?'

"He tilted his head at me, smiled that smile that he's so famous for. 'Mom says women are crazy.'

"'That they are.'

"He took a cigarette from me and lit it. 'Well, apparently this one is. How many times did she call?'

"'A bunch.'

"He puffed on his cigarette for a moment, then tilted his head and looked at me again. 'Well, I guess I dodged a bullet this time, then.' The reference to his dad was unmistakable."

I guess I must've looked skeptical at this paean to the purity of Jackson Alexander Franklin, because he said, "Make no mistake about it, Marina. Zander's not afraid of women. He knows perfectly well how he looks. He knows what the way he looks does to you." I flinched at the personal pronoun, even though he hadn't intended it personally.

"God, the things the fan girls *write*, the things they *say* to him at conventions. But he just bats those baby blues at them, and acts like he has no idea what they're talking about. *Surely you don't mean what you could be construed to mean. I am a complete stranger to you, a happily married man.* That's what his expression says.

"He's pushing forty, for Christ's sake, and he just looks at them blankly and pretends like he has no idea what they're talking about. When he's with fans, his charm is the 800 pound gorilla in the room, but he doesn't acknowledge it, so by tacit agreement, they're not supposed to acknowledge it either."

He paused again to let all this sink in. "Zander was never a pussy-hound anyway, but there would be no football for him, no proms, no dates. He was perfectly willing to stay at home, just to please Mom."

I was still skeptical. "Yet Sheila somehow slid in there."

His eyebrows went up in surprise, and he polished off the remainder of his second drink. "Indeed. Someday I'll have to tell you about how *all that* went down."

"I can't wait."

Again he showed all his teeth. "Maybe he didn't do it all for Mom. Maybe he stayed home like she'd asked because he'd just never seen anything he liked. Until *she* came along."

I didn't have anything to say to this, and I was spared from having to think something up because Greg's phone rang. He looked at it. "Speak of the devil." He pushed the button. "Yes, Master?"

I thought about all that he'd said. 800 pound gorilla, indeed. What he does to *you.*

Then Greg was handing his phone to me, and my mind went blank, *tabula rasa.* Zander wanted to talk to *me.* I found my voice, stammered out hello.

"Hey, Marina." The beloved voice, so familiar, saying *my* name. "Didn't Charlie tell me that you have bees?"

I almost said, *Who?* But then I recalled Charlie, poor hung over, couldn't hang, forgotten Charlie. "Yes," I replied. "I have some bees."

"Do you think I could come to your house and check 'em out? I'm kind of at odds and ends here." The same expression his brother had used. "Sheila feels sick, Charlie won't pick up his phone, Greg's with you."

Oh, my poor baby! I thought. "Sure," I said.

"Great. I've got a cab right here. Tell him where to bring me."

I told the cabdriver where I lived, hung up the phone, handed it back to Greg. "He wants to see my bees."

"Of course he does!" Greg smiled. He looked at my second Bloody Caesar, untouched. "No use letting this go to waste." He drank it off in one long swallow, then shuddered. "This is a great restaurant. Tastes just like home."

Greg paid the tab, slapped the maître d' on the back on the way out. We retrieved my car from the lot; I called Maria and said I would be out for the rest of the day.

TWENTY-THREE

Zander was standing on the sidewalk in front of my house with his hands in his pockets when we pulled up. Again I thought I might just die at the very lusciousness of him.

He smiled at us, clapped his brother on the back. I was all confidence now that I was in my own house. That home field advantage just washed over me. I'd taken a page out of Charlie's unwittingly feminist handbook and hired a maid service. I wouldn't be able to afford it forever, but I would figure out a way to manage to keep it I for as long as my Canadian friends were here.

So, yeah, the house was immaculate. I gave them the brief grand tour, told them a little about the American Craftsman style of architecture, bemoaned the single bathroom, and made my little quip about long barrels on Tommy guns.

Zander smiled at me, confused. Oh, great Christ, but he was adorable! How could someone who was pushing forty - as Greg had mentioned – still look *so adorable?*

I said, "You know, a Tommy gun? Gangsters? The Roaring 20's? Chicago?" He nodded. "Well, the classic Tommy gun had a short barrel. If you go to buy one new, though, they don't look like that anymore. A new Tommy gun has a long barrel. It still looks enough like a Tommy gun, but there's just something off about it."

"Like guns do you, Marina?" Greg asked.

I showed them the gun safe in the back bedroom, but made no move to open it. "They were mostly my father's," I explained.

If Zander wanted to see the guns, I would be more than happy to oblige him. But there is nothing more boring than looking at guns if one isn't into guns. And the bees, buzzing merrily, were waiting. A moment passed, and when neither of them indicated any further interest in my guns, I led them to the backyard.

All was glowing and in bloom, and I sent up another prayer of love to Uncle Pete. Zander walked slowly into the backyard, walked slowly down the little cobblestone paths. I hung back a little, watching him, reveling in the moment.

It was still all too incredible, still all so unbelievable. Jackson Alexander Franklin was in *my backyard*, in my garden, walking around, commenting on things, admiring things. He stopped and looked at us. "This is awesome!" he said simply, and my poor heart *fucking rejoiced*.

"Do you want to inspect the hives?" I asked and dared to smile at him. He smiled back at me and nodded and I said, "Everything's in the shed. I only have one suit, though." I cursed this oversight on my part, but then I guessed I'd never believed that there would ever be an occasion that I would need two suits. I'd never truly believed that I might ever be inspecting the hives with *him*.

"I'll make it quick then," he said, and dashed off toward the shed.

"If you are going to start this shit, then I need a drink, Zander!" Greg called after him.

Zander peeked around a bush, smiled mischievously, and flipped his brother off. Then he ducked into the shed. I thought I might die at the cuteness of it all, and wondered vaguely if I would ever not feel like I was going to die at Zander Franklin's cuteness. I doubted it.

Greg shook his head, looked at me. "Do you have any vodka? Clamato? Any horseradish?"

I shook my head. "There's a liquor store on the corner, about six blocks up the street. You can take my car. The keys are probably still in the door."

Zander emerged, already suited up. "Get some Grolsch," he said to his brother.

Greg shuddered, said, "Ewww. Is there anything particular you want?" he asked me. "I know you weren't impressed with the Caesars."

"Grolsch is fine," I said, although I'd never had a Grolsch in my life. Greg shuddered again and turned to go. I said, "Hey, how does a pizza sound? I've haven't eaten all day."

"Sounds great. But let me order it, okay? I like them loaded."

"No problem," I replied, and Greg left. I heard my car start, and then I forgot that he even existed. I sat on the patio in the middle of the garden, listened to the delightful splashing of Grandma's little fountain. And I watched Zander opening up my beehives, puffing the smoker, peering inside, examining a frame. I heard him exclaim over the top bar hive, even though it was empty, awaiting the next swarm.

It was the most wonderful moment of my life up to that point. The sun glinted, everything was golden and rosy. While I couldn't see his face through the netting, *I knew it was him*, and that was more than good enough. It was like an episode of *The Beekeeper* come to life, right there in my own Southern California back yard. Could anything be better than this?

TWENTY-FOUR

Way too shortly, Greg returned. He set a six-pack of Budweiser and a six-pack of Grolsch on the little table next to the fountain and handed me a cold one. I looked at the strange complicated lid on it for a second, dumbfounded. He shook his head. "It's called a *flippie*. And don't forget, you asked for it."

He took the bottle from me, held it between his palms, popped it open using both thumbs, and handed it back to me. He plopped down on another patio chair, opened a Bud, and lit a cigarette.

He watched me watch Zander. I became aware of this and looked at him. It was probably not a wise topic, but I had to ask. "Does his wife do beekeeping with him?"

He smirked in undisguised contempt. "Sheila? No. Sheila's allergic to bees. Like, deadly allergic. In fact, Sheila's allergic to a lot of things. Air that's too hot. Air that's too cold. Conventions. The air in convention centers never fails to make her sick."

I thought that it was probably the adoration of the fan girls at those conventions that made her sick. I imagined that if they were there in any numbers, the adoration would be a palpable thing, like some kind of estrogen mist.

"So, she's sickly? She doesn't look sickly."

"Oh, no, she's healthy as a horse. Except that she's allergic to all kinds of things." The subject seemed to annoy Greg, and he called to his brother, "Hey, Zander, we're in America now, for Christ's sake! Can we forget about bees for one minute? I got you some Grolsch!"

Zander flipped him off again, and it was hilarious with the beekeeper's glove. But after a few more minutes, he closed everything up, dumped out the smoker and snuffed out the burlap. He approached, pulling off the hat and veil. His skin was sweaty, his hair matted. I wanted to lick his face.

I said, "What's the verdict?"

He removed the gloves and set them on the table, put the hat down on top of them, pushed the elasticized sleeves of the bee suit up to his elbows. He picked up a Grolsch. Unlike Greg, he only needed one hand to open the flippie, carelessly placing one finger on either side of the wires and popping it open. He did it absent-mindedly, without even looking at it.

"Your hives look great. The bees are beautiful." He looked a long swig on his beer, and then kicked his brother in the foot. "God damn, but this is good beer!"

Greg smiled. "You're nuts."

I looked at the bottle and asked them, "Is this Canadian beer?"

"No," Greg said. "It's supposedly Dutch beer. But they're a sponsor of the Toronto International Film Festival. He appeared there last year, and -"

"And the Grolsch rep hooked me up!" Zander said. He sat in the other patio chair and stretched his long legs out in front of him.

"She sends him like ten cases a month," Greg said. "You don't have to drink it, you know, just because they send it to you. And you really don't have to drink it here."

"But I like it!" Zander insisted.

"It's terrible," Greg replied.

It *was* terrible, but it had just become my beer of choice.

TWENTY-FIVE

Greg had bought a case of Budweiser in addition to the six pack. Apparently Grolsch didn't come in anything but sixers, so he'd bought five of them. My refrigerator was stuffed. Some drinkers were these Canadians.

I called the pizza place and told them the address, then handed the phone to Greg so he could order his loaded pies. When he went out front to wait for the delivery guy, I was left alone with Zander, sitting there next to me, for the very first time. I would not be disappointed.

He said, "This place is great, Marina." He gestured at our surroundings. "The house, the garden, everything. I love it."

It's yours, I thought. *Let me get a pen. I'll sign it over to you.*

"It's really peaceful," he continued. "You'd never know that you were in the middle of town."

"This isn't much of a town," I said, "We're fifty miles from LA. That's too far for this to be much of a town."

"I've been to LA a couple of times. I didn't care for it."

I didn't really care for LA too much either, so I said, "Don't you live on a farm or something?"

"Nah," he said, the regret in his voice a tangible thing. "My parents do." He examined the flippie on his Grolsch. "We live in the city. Close to the action and all."

"Well, you can visit all you want while you're here," I said, thinking it sounded lame as soon as I said it.

But Zander looked at me over his beer; he smiled and those blue eyes pierced me to the soul. "That's very kind of you. I most definitely will take you up on it."

Surely, I was imagining a certain affectionate look in his eyes. Surely, I was just wishing that it was there?

He continued, "We were going to stay with Charlie, but Sheila said that we'd be intruding now that he had a girlfriend, so -"

"I'm not really Charlie's . . . What I mean is, we haven't really been seeing each other that long. It's not at all a serious thing."

There it was again, that little glint in his eye, a little crooked half smile this time, like he was glad to hear me deny Charlie. I had to be imagining it.

He shrugged. "It doesn't matter. He wasn't expecting *three* of us. And the hotel is fine. Sheila and Greg, they love hotels, anyway. They haven't stayed in as many of them as I have."

Just then, Greg returned with three pizza boxes. Zander grabbed gloves, hat and veil from where he'd tossed them on the table, so Greg could set the pizzas down. "I guess I should change out of this." He walked over and retrieved the smoker from where he'd left it by the hives, and walked back to the shed. It was like another scene from *The Beekeeper.*

Greg said, "Plates?"

I blinked at him. "Oh. Top shelf on the left. As you walk in the door."

TWENTY-SIX

So we ate pizza and got mellowly drunk again, my two favorite Canadians and I. Charlie called three times; I ignored him.

Sheila called once. Zander said to me, "She wants to know - here." He handed me his phone.

Sheila sounded all snuffly and congested when she said, "Hi, Marina. Sorry I'm sick."

"Oh, it's okay, honey," I replied, proud of the concern with which I colored my voice. "You just take care of yourself and get better." *And I'll take care of your gorgeous husband for you, as much as he will let me,* I thought.

"It'll pass," she was saying. "I was wondering if you might want to go shopping tomorrow?"

"Sure, honey," I said. "If you're feeling better." *If you don't just do us all a great big favor and* fucking die, I thought.

"Great!" she said, and coughed a little. "Give Jake your number so he can put it in his phone."

"Okay, I will. You take care of yourself now." I handed the phone back to her husband.

He said to her, "Okay, I will. I'll see you later. Love you, too," and pushed the disconnect button. Then he said to me, "What's your number, Marina?" and for a full count of ten I couldn't remember it. At last my brain connected. He entered my number into his phone, and immediately my phone trilled, sitting there on the table among the empties and pizza detritus. "Now you have mine, too."

Greg said, "Don't leave me out of the phone fest." He looked at me, and I repeated my number. He put it in his phone, and again the little electronic wonder lit up and rang.

I could die happy, now. I not only had Jackson Alexander Franklin's cell phone number, I had his manager's, too. *CanadaBees* could just eat her heart out.

We talked and laughed and drank. Occasionally, I would look at my phone sitting there on the little table, but I couldn't bear to pick it up, thinking that I would somehow accidentally, drunkenly erase the precious numbers. But then Charlie called again, and I had to pick it up to press *Ignore* once more.

At last it was time for them to go back to the hotel. I apologized for being too drunk to drive them there, but Zander had the cab company's number in his phone. He called and the three of us staggered out to the sidewalk to wait.

When the cab pulled up, Greg gave me a big sloppy hug, and his customary kiss on the cheek. He was what one calls *falling down drunk*. "Talk to you soon," he slurred, then opened the door and slid gracelessly into the back seat. I leaned over and waved to him.

I stood up and turned around, and Jackson Alexander Franklin was standing there, waiting for me. *Zander*, my mind breathed. He gave me that little half smile again, and opened his arms, offering me a hug.

I did not hesitate, my brothers and only friends. I was drunk and here was something that I'd dreamed of for my entire life. But I had to take it slow, lest I lose my self-control, lest I launch myself into his arms and cling to him desperately and then have to be physically removed before I would let go.

I took a step forward, ever so slowly, into his embrace. He hugged me to him and I smelled beer and cigarettes, but also the wonderful scent of him. He smelled *sooo good!* I hugged him back and it was everything I'd always imagined it would be, and seemed to last a glorious eternity. But at last, with my last shred of self-control, I stepped back.

He touched my cheek, then, and said, "Thanks for entertaining us all afternoon, Marina. I had a lot of fun."

I looked back into the beloved blue eyes for a second, then looked away, knowing if I held his gaze a second more, that lifetime of longing would spill out.

Then I looked back at him again and smiled. "Anytime, Zander. I had a great time, too."

He continued to look at me, seemed like he wanted to say something else, but I must've been imagining it.

Greg said, "For God's sake, Zander, get in the fucking car! I need to get some sleep."

TWENTY-SEVEN

Mercifully, the next day was Saturday, and I'd be able to sleep in. *Ah, sleep! Innocent sleep/Sleep that knits up the ravell'd sleeve of care/The death of each day's life . . . Chief nourisher in life's feast.*

And I really needed it, to throw off the consequences of the rollercoaster of an emotional and alcoholic binge that I'd been riding for the last couple of days. Hot damn, but these Canadians could drink! I hadn't imbibed like this since my college days. And I was so much younger then, when the aftereffects of any sin were thrown off by the mind and body so carelessly, so completely, gone by the next sunrise.

But it was not to be. No sleeping in, no much needed healing for me on that Saturday. At 9:30, my phone rang. I rolled over, thinking that if this was Charlie, no punishment would suffice. I would simply have to kill him.

But the delightful little pixels on the screen spelled out *Zander*, and I snapped immediately to complete wakefulness. I put a smile in my voice, pushed the button and said hello.

But it wasn't Zander. It was Sheila, sounding all fresh and cheerful, all trace of her sniffles gone. She was asking me if I still wanted to go shopping. I told her that I would be delighted, that I would be there to pick her up at the hotel in an hour.

"Great! Just call when you get here and I'll come down." She paused. "Let me call you back on my phone, so you have the number. This is Zander's phone, and he's still asleep." Like I didn't already know both of these things.

She did as she'd explained; I answered the new number and she bubbled, "Hi! Me again! See you soon!"

I wanted to just stand there in the shower all morning, attempting to let the hot water wash the drunk out of me, but it was not to be. I had to make it a quick one, if I was going to make it over there in an hour.

At first, I dreaded the entire thing, spending the whole day with *her*. I wondered if I could successfully fight the urge to stab her through the heart and just leave her to bleed out in Macy's changing room. But as I put on my face (oh, God, the dark circles! I looked like a fucking raccoon!), my mind began to change. Curiosity began to assert itself.

It would be interesting in a perverse sort of way to get to know his wife, wouldn't it? What new insider information could be gained, what further insights into his opinions, his habits, his likes and dislikes? What tidbits about his plans for the future?

So by the time I pulled up to the hotel, I was intrigued by all the possibilities. I looked at her name on my phone and hit the button. At first, I'd downloaded a kangaroo for her contact picture, then decided, no, that was just rude, what if someone should see it? Then I put up a map of Australia to represent her, like the original mnemonic I'd come up with. But that seemed somehow disrespectful too (if anyone should see it), so I finally just went with her name, sans any picture. I'd put an innocent honeybee for Zander's contact picture, and just to be contrary, a Grolsch logo for Greg's.

Just as she had sounded on the phone, Sheila was fresh and perky, and *so* glad to see me. I drove to the mall, and we walked around, just window-shopping for a minute. I thought for a second that she was going to enter the Victoria's Secret, and I decided that I would definitely just have to stab her then, if she made me watch her pick out lingerie to wear for the man I loved.

Fortunately for her, she passed the nightie store by, then turned to me and said, "Are you hungry? They say you're not supposed to shop on an empty stomach."

I couldn't tell if she was kidding or not, thinking, *you're not supposed to* shop for groceries *on an empty stomach, you twit.* I should eat something; I knew it, for my health's sake. But my stomach felt as though it had been surgically removed, laid out on hot asphalt and beat with a meat tenderizer. Then a couple of Bloody Caesars (with extra horseradish) had been poured all over it, and then it had been reinserted by a surgeon with dirty fingernails. In other words, I wasn't even a little bit hungry.

Sheila stood in the food court like the stereotypical kid in a candy store, looking at all the choices, seeking something uniquely American, I guess. Apparently, they didn't have *Hot Dog On A Stick* in the Great White North, because that was what she finally decided on. *You won't stay all rosy-cheeked and peaches and cream complected for long, eating that shit,* I thought, as my stomach rolled over. I hit the Starbucks. They had Starbucks in Canada, and Sheila didn't want any this time.

I sipped the hot, sweet, blessed caffeine, and tried not to be too disgusted watching her devour her hot dog on a stick. I wanted to ask her about her relationship with Zander, how it was all going after twenty long years of marriage, but I feared my own curiosity, feared that I might ask the wrong questions, offend her in some way, put her on her guard.

But fortunately, she threw out the opening girl-talk gambit by asking, "So how is everything going between you and my brother?"

"As best as can be expected, I guess," I said truthfully. *Seeing as he's nothing but a tool to me,* I thought.

"He really likes you," she said. No revelation there. She paused, then suddenly said, "Do you want kids?"

I barked a little laugh before I could stop myself. "Kids? I'm thirty-five, Sheila. That's a little old to start thinking about kids."

I looked at her crestfallen expression, and suddenly recalled that I'd read somewhere (*CanadaBees'* blog no doubt), that she was two years younger than Zander, which would make her thirty-six. *Oh, shit, wrong answer!* So I said gently, "Do *you* want kids?

"Like you say, it's getting a little late for all that."

Her sad expression, completely unexpected, should've evoked some pity in me, and I'm sure that it would have, if it was possible for me to feel any pity at all for *the most fortunate woman in the world.*

"You could adopt," I suggested, imagining what a PR coup that would be. Maybe they could adopt the orphaned kid of a dead beekeeper or something.

"Jake doesn't want any kids," she said flatly, and I thought, *could I possibly love him more?*

Because I didn't want any kids either. The very idea turned my stomach, even when I wasn't nursing a binge-drinking hangover. One more symptom of my own unnaturalness, perhaps. Not only no, but *hell, no.*

"I'm sorry to hear that, for your sake, Sheila," I said.

Her shoulders moved up and down, as if to say, *What are you gonna do?* and I thought, *Oh, yeah, you just go right ahead and shrug it off, you bitch; not having children is certainly a small price to pay in order to stay married to him. I would sacrifice damn near anything, right arms, kidneys; I would give my front seat in hell to be in your shoes.*

She sighed, and I asked, even more gently, "Is that why you seem so sad?"

She smiled gamely now, the little trouper. "Ah, no, the kid thing, that's a long standing issue. Nothing to be done, no reason to be sad about it. If I seem sad now, it's probably because I'm homesick." She absently twirled the *Hot Dog On A Stick* skewer, then tossed it onto the plate. "I really hate to travel, period, but it's not so bad when we're in Canada. My allergies always act up so terribly when we leave the country."

"Bad, are they?"

"Oh, you have no idea. I sneeze, my eyes run. I get all stuffed up and puffy. Hives, sometimes. It's a mess."

Still I could summon up not one scintilla of pity for her. They had medication for that kind of thing, did they not? Once again, I thought it was all but a small price to pay to be by his side.

"I've actually been thinking about going back home, at least until filming actually starts on this thing."

Hope flared in my heart like a Roman candle. "I think that's a great idea, Sheila. Go home, rest, heal."

She smiled at me, and said, "Oh, Jake would never go for it." Again I hated her utterly. "He's having too much fun, drinking with his brother, sleeping in."

"They *do* drink," I commented.

"You noticed that?" She smiled. "Yes, they do. But it's only because there is nothing else to do right now. They play hard -" the cliché made me cringe "- but when it's time to work, they're all business, all professionalism, all devotion to the task at hand." She sighed again. "But enough of this depressing talk. Let's shop!"

I started off with the shopping cheerfully enough, my heart buoyed up by the unhappiness in her marriage, small though it was.

TWENTY-EIGHT

We shopped, and I grew quite bored. I featured myself to be very much the martyr for putting up with her. When we were *finally* on the way back from the mall, she called her husband, and he was dutifully standing there under the hotel's canopied entrance, waiting for our arrival.

I thought I detected that little affectionate half-smile again, just for me, when our eyes met as I pulled up. But I put it down to too much drinking, not enough sleep; just plain old wishful thinking. Jackson Alexander Franklin and the 800 pound gorilla of his charm simply were not flirting with me. It just was not possible.

I popped the trunk. Sheila and I got out; she walked behind the car and hugged her husband, kissed him lightly on that flawless mouth. I didn't have time to dwell on all *that*, because my phone rang. I looked at it, prepared to ignore Charlie again.

But it was Uncle Pete. I answered it and gleefully said hi to him. "How's it going?" He asked me. "Did your Canadian boy make it in all right?"

"He did indeed, Uncle Pete," I said. "In fact, he's standing right here."

"I was wondering when you were planning to bring him out and show him my bees," he said, a little edge of feeling-left-out detectable in his voice. "I was thinking, surely he would be more impressed with a real set-up. More so than with just those three hives we stuck at your place." *Oh, my God, Uncle Pete!* I thought. *I love you!* Why had I not thought of this myself?

"I'm sure he would," I said, watching Zander unloading the voluminous number of gaily-colored shopping bags from my trunk and stacking them onto a convenient hotel luggage rack. "When would be good for you?"

"Today, tomorrow. Either way. Your aunt is working at the church rummage sale this weekend, and I don't feel much like running the stand by myself."

"I'll ask him, Uncle Pete, and then I'll call you back." He said okay and I disconnected. I watched Zander and Sheila for another moment, thinking, how had I failed to think of this myself? Then Sheila slammed the trunk of my car and they started pushing the overloaded gurney toward the entrance to the hotel. I said his name, but it only came out as a croaky whisper. I cleared my throat and said, "*Zander.*"

I was pretty sure that I couldn't lose. If not today, then tomorrow. *If it be now, 'tis not to come; if it be not to come, it will be now; if it be not now, yet it will come: the readiness is all.* And was I not more than ready to spend another day with Jackson Alexander Franklin? Greg was still sleeping it off, probably. And Sheila - wouldn't the pollen-laden fresh air of the Southern Californian, American-not-Canadian countryside play havoc with her allergies? I was pretty sure I couldn't lose. He stopped, turned, smiled at me again. Yes, I had to be imagining it; this was not a special smile, just for me. It was all in my head. Just wishful thinking.

Sheila continued through the doors of the hotel with her treasures. I walked over to where he was, and said, "That was my Uncle Pete on the phone. I don't know if I've mentioned him to you. He owns an orange grove, a fruit stand. He raises bees commercially. That's where I got my hives. I told him about you," I hurried over this little admission, adding quickly, "and he said he'd love to have a fellow beekeeper come over and check out his operation."

That glorious, Canada-famous smile bloomed. "*Uh, let me go in and ask my wife,*" he said, doing his best George Thorogood impression. The next line of song played immediately in my mind: *He came outta the house/I could see in his face/I knowed it was* - yessss! "Sheila doesn't want to go," he said, shrugging like he would've been surprised if she *had* wanted to go. "Let's do it."

TWENTY-NINE

If my not-to-be-believed interaction with Jackson Alexander Franklin up to that point had been superb, the afternoon spent at Uncle Pete's surmounted it as nothing else (well, *almost* nothing else) could. All we talked about was bees: honey-production and extraction. Hive-transport-for-pollination practices in America and Canada. And again, the tragedy of Colony Collapse Disorder, mites and viruses, what was and wasn't being done in both countries.

And I was right up there with these professionals, participating seamlessly in the discussion. I made Uncle Pete forget that he'd mostly coached me, because I'd done my own independent research online, and had opinions and ideas that he hadn't considered. I could tell he was impressed. I watched them sometimes, the old California farmer in his overalls (I kid you not); the youngish Canadian actor in his Ray-Bans, equals in their concern for the plight of the bees. It was awesome.

The only blemish on the day was when Charlie called, while we were standing out by the hives. He'd somehow summoned up the nerve to be angry. Quite angry, in fact. "Where the fuck have you been?" he asked.

"I don't think I like your tone," I said, glancing at Zander. I noted that he was listening, watching me over his sunglasses.

"I've called you like a thousand times," Charlie was saying.

I stepped away from them, feigning a desire for privacy; but not far enough away that Zander couldn't hear me. I said, "I'm sorry, Charlie," the almost-rhyme sounding so funny in my ear that I thought I might bust up. "But you don't own me." Another cliché, and I had the last one lined up already. I lowered my voice, but again, not low enough that Zander couldn't hear me. "In fact, I've been doing some soul-searching the last couple days. I think we've been moving too fast. I need a little time, a little space. I'll see you at the office on Monday."

Before he could react, say a word, I hit the disconnect, turned my phone off. There wasn't anyone that was going to call me that I wanted to talk to. The only person I wanted to talk to was right here.

I glanced at him. He smiled that little crooked grin at me, and if it was as significant as it seemed to be, I would've died right there. But I had to be imagining it.

He pushed his shades up on his nose, and turned to pay attention to something Uncle Pete was saying. Regardless of these strange tricks my mind was playing, I was glad that he'd heard me end it with Charlie.

As I watched Zander and Uncle Pete shake hands, as we said our good-byes, I was confident that my friendship with Zander was now well cemented. *Like a beehive frame cemented with propolis,* I thought, and grinned at my own cleverness.

THIRTY

As soon as we were back on the road, Zander said, "Do you barbeque?"

"I *have* a barbeque," I replied. *I knew about bees*; I didn't have to try to feign that I knew how to cook, too.

"Greg knows how to barbeque." He grinned and dialed his phone. "Hey," he said when his brother answered. "Find a grocery store. We're going to barbeque at Marina's. We'll show her how we do it in Canada. Get something that won't make Sheila break out." He paused. "Oh, yeah?" He pushed the speakerphone button. "Say that again."

"I said, Sheila's over at Charlie's house. He's all upset." I could hear the laughter in Greg's voice. "I guess Marina broke up with him over the phone."

"What a shame," Zander said, grinning at me.

I grinned back at him. "I told you that there was not one thing serious about it."

I was on Cloud 9, as the saying goes. Dave Edmunds sang in my head: *Everything is good as it pos-si-bul-ly could be.* Here I was, joking with Zander about dumping my boring boyfriend. It was like we were friends.

"Yeah, it's a crying shame," Greg was saying. "At least he's crying about it. Sheila went over there to comfort him. She called a little while ago, said he was drinking, too. She said to tell you it looked like it was going to be a bumpy night, and not to wait up for her."

"Oh, well," Zander said. "No barbeque for her then. We should be back in about -?"

"Forty-five minutes or so," I supplied.

"It'll be getting dark by then, Zander," Greg said.

"Tell him that he can go over to the house as soon as he gets the food," I said. "There's a key under the green flowerpot on the front porch."

Greg heard me. "My condolences on the end of your relationship," he said, no condolence in his voice at all.

"Shit happens," I said.

And then, meine damen und herren, mesdames et messieurs, ladies and gentlemen, I swear to God, Jackson Alexander Franklin put his fist to his mouth and *fucking giggled*. It was awesome.

"It'll be on the grill cooking when you get here," Greg said.

"Get some more Grolsch," Zander told him.

"Oh, fuck you!" Greg replied and hung up.

THIRTY-ONE

Greg had found all the light switches; the backyard was lit up and redolent with the mouth-watering smells of carnivorous cooking when we arrived. He'd located my grandma's giant ice tea pitcher and mixed himself a king-sized batch of Bloody Caesars. It was already half empty, I noted. A brand new cooler sat next to the fountain, open and overflowing with ice and Grolsch beer. Things apparently weren't that much different in Canada than they were here: it was now party time.

When he saw us, he said, "Hey!" and gestured with the spatula, walked over and clapped his brother on the shoulder with one arm and hugged me with the other. "I knew you'd get tired of Charlie." I shrugged and we all grinned at each other, then Greg shook his head and said, "You're something."

"She's something else!" Zander said with enthusiasm, and then launched into a glowing description of our glowing day at Uncle Pete's, telling his brother about everything we talked about. "The lady knows her shit," he concluded.

Greg tilted his head and squinted at me. "How'd you learn so much about bees?" he asked, and I detected a trace of what one could almost call *suspicion* in his voice.

But I was too happy for the moment to worry about my secret love for Zander being exposed, and I figured I was probably just imagining the suspicion, just like I was imagining Zander making eyes at me. I slapped him on the arm, and replied, "It's a family business!"

Then Zander said, "When do we eat?"

Greg stopped looking at me, said, "Oh, shit!" and sprinted back to the smoking barbeque.

THIRTY-TWO

While I'm by no means any kind of barbeque aficionado, I had to admit that the Canadian way did taste different than any other barbeque that I'd ever had. And it was delicious.

We laughed and drank and ate. That little part of my brain that always remained sober (call it my self-control) observed that there seemed to be a lot more touching going on now between Zander and myself, and warned that I'd best watch it. Yes, he would touch my shoulder or my back; even put his arm around my waist or my neck. I was careful to make sure that I didn't touch him back. At least not too much.

I put it down to drink and lack of adult supervision, because Greg was touchy too, also putting his arm around my waist a couple of times. There was nothing else to it. Reading anything else into would be to give in to my fantasies, just the thing that my self-control was there to prevent. Besides, this was all wondrous enough as it was, and I thought that I would just be being greedy to wish for anything more.

The beers in the cooler waned, but I knew that there were plenty more in the fridge. Greg Franklin did not fuck around when it came to having enough to drink on hand. He made himself another pitcher of Bloody Caesars and not long after that the conversation turned to music.

Then nothing was to be done but for the three of us to lurch into the house so I could regale them with American music. My iPod was at work; but the laptop was sitting on the desk, so I just hooked it up to my not unimpressive sound system, and the rocking out commenced. I was too drunk to worry about offending their Canadian sensibilities with stuff they'd not heard before. I have to admit, though, it was hard to find any consensus on the newer stuff.

But I wasn't worried. I have extraordinarily eclectic taste in music, if I do say so myself, and it soon became karaoke night when I turned the clock back a few decades.

The three of us sang along raucously (and more than a little off key) when the shuffle played Norman Greenbaum's *Spirit in the Sky*, and Three Dog Night's *Mama Told Me Not To Come*. This went on for some time, and we had a blast; Greg giggled hysterically when Zander sang along to Lonesome George's *One Bourbon, One Scotch, One Beer*, and *I Drink Alone*.

But when he did *Bad to The Bone*, it was simply not to be believed. First he sang, *I broke a thousand hearts/Before I met you*, directly to me, looking me right in the eye. *I'll break a thousand more, baby/Before I am through*. I heard again the delectable darkness in his voice. Then he just let the 800 pound gorilla run fucking loose, singing: *I make a rich woman beg/I'll make a good woman steal/I'll make an old woman blush/and make a young girl squeal*.

Jackson Alexander Franklin grinned, then, because no man could achieve all of this quicker, better, and more completely than he could. And *nobody* – not me, not *CanadaBees*, not Greg – knew it better than Zander himself did. A little ego is permissible, I thought, when a man looked as incredible as he did.

When the *oldie* oldies part of the queue rolled on, the three of us joined arms and did a chorus line kick to Sinatra's *New York, New York*. Then, when the horns started on fellow Rat Packer Dean Martin's *Sway*, Zander released Greg (he'd been in the middle, between the two of us), swung around and grabbed me by the hand, pulled me to him, and said, "Tell me, Marina. Do you know how to rumba?"

"As a matter of fact, I do, Zander," I replied, thanking my mother again for all those dance lessons in middle school, and the grands for the enormous living room of their Craftsman house, more than suitable for dancing. We were both a little rusty, and much more than a little drunk, but I didn't fall when he twirled me, and he didn't drop me when we dipped.

Next we did a nice lively step to Lena Horne singing *Stormy Weather*. I looked over and noticed that Greg had quite passed out on the couch. I nodded at him, and Zander just smiled, not missing a step. Our dancing got more in sync as the song progressed. It was all effortless for Zander, and you know what they say about a man who knows how to dance. If you don't know what they say, then I feel sorry for you. Google it.

Then The Platters' *Twilight Time* came on, and Zander pulled me closer to him and slowed it down a little bit. It's a terrible thing to admit, my brothers and only friends, but I'd become so accustomed to him holding me close while we danced, that I forgot to obsess about it, forgot to think that it couldn't possibly be happening, forgot to think that I might just die. The anxiety had evaporated. I just let it all go and enjoyed the complete arousal that dancing with him produced. But I didn't *think* about it.

We sang along with the Platters, and it seemed the most natural thing in the world, when on the last long tone, Zander took my face in both hands and kissed me.

I put my arms around his neck and we kissed through the opening bars of *I Left my Heart in San Francisco*, all the way until Tony started singing, *I'm going home to my city by the bay*. Then Zander stopped kissing me, tilted his head and gave me that little crooked half-smile. He winked then, and I realized that I hadn't been imagining it after all. I smiled back at him.

The thought of what it all could possibly mean did not enter my head. Like I say, it seemed like the most natural thing in the world, just a moment to be lived. We clung together like teenagers at one of those proms he never attended, singing *I Left my Heart in San Francisco* to each other. And when Tony sang *above the blue and windy sea*, he kissed me again, finishing on the final cymbal splash.

Then we opened our eyes and just looked at each other for the seconds before Anita Ward's disco anthem, *Ring My Bell* started. Zander yelped, "Whooooo!" waking Greg up. He spun me around, and never letting go of my hand, he showed me his best *Saturday Night Fever* stylings, singing in falsetto to *Ring My Bell*. Then we danced to *Brick House*: a little Bump, a little Hustle. A little Electric Slide.

While we danced to The Commodores, I looked at Greg, now sitting up and blinking. I watched him find his drink, watched him retrieve his phone from the coffee table and look at it. I could tell it was ringing because it lit up, even though I couldn't hear it over the music. I watched him push what I could only assume was the *Ignore* button, and then look up at Zander.

When the song ended, he said. "Time to go, John Travolta. Your responsibilities are calling." I let go of Zander's hand and quickly muted the iTunes.

Zander looked at his brother, his expression unreadable; Greg shrugged and made that little *What are you going to do?* expression in reply.

I looked at the clock. It was 2:30. I said, "It *is* late."

Zander looked at me with that now familiar affectionate smile, that one that I'd been denying. I smiled back at him, and then he took his phone out of his pocket and called the cab company again. I imagined that their cab fare bills must be astronomical. But on the other hand, I'd also noticed that the one thing that they didn't seem to be lacking was money.

It was almost an exact repeat of the night before. The cab showed up, Greg gave me a hug and a kiss on the cheek, told me he would see me soon, and slid gracelessly into the backseat of the cab. Again, he was what one calls *falling down drunk*.

But I didn't waste any time with leaning over and waving goodbye to him this time. I turned to Zander and he hugged me, squeezed me, picked me up off my feet. Then he took my face in both hands again and kissed me quickly on the forehead. "I'll talk to you tomorrow," he said softly. Then he slid in the cab before Greg could start bitching again and they were gone.

I would like to tell you, my pedigree chums, that I climbed into bed and congratulated myself, commended myself on the fact that all my devious little plots and machinations had paid off in spades, in ways that I'd never dared to even imagine. But I was drunk, for an uncharacteristic third night in a row, and when I slid between the sheets I was asleep, as they say, before my head hit the pillow.

THIRTY-THREE

My phone buzzed at 11 the next morning. Zander texted: *Still sleeping?*

I wrote back: *Pretty much.*

He wrote: *Me too. Talk to you later. Had a great time.*

I replied: *Me, too.*

I had just enough time to think for a second about how dangerous *all that* was, before I drifted back to sleep again.

I stayed in bed the whole day. The headache didn't seem so bad if I was lying down. I just lay there, perfectly calm, perfectly at peace, remembering what it was like to dance with him. For probably the first time since I'd clapped peepers on Jackson Alexander Franklin, courtesy of *Netflix*, I wasn't consumed by that hurts-so-good anxiety, that longing that's so painful and so wonderful. Unrequited, unrequitable. It didn't matter right then. I didn't plan or plot, didn't think about the future, didn't think about the reality of the situation, didn't think about his wife, didn't think about what it all meant, what could happen next.

I just remembered. The way he smelled, the feel of his body against mine when we danced, the way he smiled, the way his mouth felt and tasted when he kissed me. It had all been *so good*.

I felt that, if I never saw him again . . . Although I knew that I would, so that's not exactly right. Let me start over. I felt that, if he never held me in his arms again, it would still be all right, because I'd already danced with him, kissed him. And that was more than I could've ever asked for, more than I'd ever really believed would ever happen. It was enough. *Mellow is the man/Who knows what he's been missing.*

At three o'clock, Zander texted me: *What r u doin?*

Just laying around, fighting this hangover. Not winning. What r u doin?

Hanging out by the pool, trying to bake out the Grolschs.

I shuddered. The sun was the enemy when I had a hangover. No shades were dark enough to prevent its rays from piercing my brain. Better to hide from the sun, stay in a dark room until the results of alcohol abuse dissipated.

Zander texted again: *Charlie's here. Hungover, not saying much. Think Greg might b dead. Hasn't moved in a while. He's getting sunburnt. Bout time to push him into the pool.*

I smiled. My silly Canadian friends. *Do it!*

No; he'd kill me. Studio execs will be here 2morrow @ 3. Charlie wants us there at 1 to get all ducks in a row b4 they show. Will u b there?

Oh, fuck, I thought. There was no reason for me to be there. I really didn't have anything to do with the whole action, nothing whatsoever; no need for a paralegal to be involved, especially not me. And there was no reason for Charlie to invite me to sit in on the meeting, seeing how I'd phone-call dumped him, broke his heart. This burnt bridge would have to be rebuilt, at least partially, and fast.

I texted back: *Prolly.*

Great!

I read back over his texts, decided that they weren't so dangerous after all. Nothing but stuff friends would say to each other. I typed: *C u there.*

Then I called Charlie. Time to make it all better. As the phone rang, I pictured them all sitting around the hotel pool, the hungover men slumped in their chairs, Sheila probably all perky, playing games on her phone or something. Pale Canadians wearing sunglasses. Except for Greg, who was getting sunburnt.

Charlie said hello. His tone of voice wasn't recriminating or bitter, but had quite the hopeful cast to it. This was good.

I said, "Look, Charlie, I want to apologize. I want to explain." He didn't say anything, but I heard an abrupt scraping sound. That would be him getting up from his chair by the pool, walking away to where his relatives couldn't hear him.

I continued. "The fact is, I just got scared, Charlie." Oh, this was just too much. "We've only been seeing each other for a couple of months . . . And everything, everything has moved so fast. My feelings . . . Everything has moved so fast, and I got scared."

Still he didn't say anything; I imagined that he might be *afraid* to say anything, afraid that if he spoke, he might somehow mess up this totally unexpected bid at reconciliation.

I said, "Do you think we could start over? Start from the beginning again, like nothing ever happened? Do you think we could just start out being friends again?"

"Whatever you want, Marina," he croaked out in delighted relief. "I'm sorry if I moved too fast." That's right, Charlie, blame it on yourself. It was all your fault.

"Okay, I'm glad that it's all settled. I'm glad we're friends again. I'll see you at work tomorrow."

He said he would see me tomorrow and hung up.

A few minutes later, I got a text from Sheila: *So glad u & Charlie are getting back 2gether!*

Shit, I thought. *Fucking Charlie.*

Then Zander texted: *What did u say 2 Charlie? He just jumped into the pool.*

I thought a minute. I didn't want Zander reading anything into stupid Charlie's stupid behavior. Didn't want him to think what Sheila did. So I wrote: *Just thinking about ur meeting 2morrow. Don't want Charlie 2 b sad. Want him 2 bring his A game. So I asked if we could still b friends.*

Zander sent a smiley face, then: *Ur something else.*

I most certainly am, I thought. I typed: *Thnx.*

THIRTY-FOUR

I finally dragged myself out of bed. I opened my not insubstantial closet and started prospecting. I had to be flawlessly turned-out tomorrow. I was going to be meeting with Hollywood studio executives. Even though I probably wouldn't say a word (I really had no business being there, after all) I would still be representing the firm. And myself. I had to look like a million bucks, tax free.

I selected my favorite black suit, the one with the tiny, almost undetectable charcoal gray pinstripes. The cut was excellent, form fitting, the skirt just a shade shorter than most of my business attire, hitting me just in the middle of the knee. I knew I looked great in this outfit. Satisfied, I hung it on the door and went downstairs.

On the way down the steps, I shuddered at the prospect of the mess we'd left the night before: mounds of dirty dishes, a dead army of empty beer bottles. Stinky, overflowing ashtrays. Zander and Greg smoked almost as much as they drank, and I'd joined them. Yuck, what a mess.

But when I walked into the living room, all was in sparkling, fresh-smelling order. I'd forgotten about the maid service. They'd already been there, while I lounged around in bed all day, like someone who could afford them. I wasn't surprised that I hadn't heard them, because like I've said, the plaster walls in the old Craftsman do a pretty good job at muffling sound. And I had undoubtedly dozed quite a bit, too.

Satisfied at the wonderful things that money could buy, I ran myself a nice bubble bath. I climbed into the tub, and stretched out in the fragrant hot water. I thought about Zander again. I just relaxed there in the tub, remembering the delightful evening we'd spent together, until the water grew cold and the shadows grew long. *Heavenly shades of night are falling/It's twilight time.*

THIRTY-FIVE

I was at my desk bright and early the next morning, feeling great; all traces of the aftereffects of binge drinking with Canadians were gone. I almost eagerly started in on the mountain of work. There was a lot of it; it seemed like I'd not hit a lick in days. My mind had been somewhere else.

Charlie showed up in my doorway at nine. He looked a little worse for wear, mostly around the eyes. But I could tell that he was happy, hopeful again. He said, "Friends?" I favored him with my friendliest smile and nodded. "Jake and Greg are going to be here at one. We're going to have to hammer this one out quickly; the studio boys will be here at three. I know it's not strictly kosher," I inwardly shuddered at yet another cliché, "but you're welcome to sit in. Bill it to overhead."

"Sounds great," I said, thinking I'd been billing a lot to overhead lately.

Charlie smiled his hopeful, happy little smile again, and went back to his office. I actually got a lot of work done, didn't let the sound of the elevator dinging back into my perception until about 12:30.

At 12:50, I was standing at the file cabinet in my office. The elevator dinged and I looked up; they stepped off the elevator and started their slow motion stroll up the short hall. It seemed in slow motion to me, still, familiarity not having dulled my appreciation of watching the two of them walk by.

Zander wore a dark gray suit, a black shirt, and a light, almost electric blue tie. Greg wore a dark brown suit, a white shirt, and a black tie. Linda, who happened to be walking by again, who I'd forgotten about entirely, actually turned around and looked at them this time. I picked a pen off my desk and wrote *Basement* on a Post-It, then stuck it on the corner of my computer.

They walked up to reception. Greg spoke to Maria, but Zander just looked at me across the office. I was glad I was standing up, so he could take in the full effect. He didn't smile for a second, just looked appreciatively at me. Did I not say that I looked like a million bucks in that black suit? Then he smiled a little surprised half grin and looked at his shoes, realizing that he'd been staring at me. He looked up when Greg motioned him forward.

Charlie came up the short hall to meet them, and Zander waved at me as they passed by. Then Greg stuck his head back in my office door, smiled his shark's grin and said, "Aren't you coming?"

I smiled back, and said, "Honey, I'm not even breathing hard."

He laughed at that one, and the two of us walked together down the hall to Charlie's office. Charlie picked up a stuffed accordion folder from his desk and suggested that we go upstairs to the main conference room.

We sat at the large conference table: I sat next to Charlie, facing the glass wall that let out into the hall where the elevators were. Zander and Greg sat across from us. Charlie handed out copies of the contract. It was straightforward, except that the studio seemed to be in rather a hurry to get this show on the road, so to speak. If he agreed to the terms, Zander was supposed to be in LA in seven days. *Damn,* I thought, *the ink won't even be dry by then.*

Charlie went over the contract, point by point. True, the schedule would be tight, but the compensation was more than generous for someone who was totally unknown in the States.

Contract law and contracts in general are unbelievably boring, and after awhile I just listened to the drone of Charlie's voice without hearing his words, and looked at Zander and Greg. They both looked shiny and new, bright-eyed and bushy-tailed, even. I remembered what Sheila had said about their being professional when it came time to be professional. They certainly looked the part now.

One would never guess that Greg had passed out on my couch two nights before, one would never guess that Zander and I had drunkenly danced and . . . made out. He looked across the table at me just as that thought crossed my mind, and smiled at me curiously. I looked away, then looked back at him, then he looked away and pretended to be listening to Charlie. I got the wonderful impression that we'd been thinking about the same thing at the same time.

Everything was in order. However, Zander said that he wasn't in love with the day after tomorrow production schedule.

"They're firm on that," Charlie said. "Something about fiscal budget."

Zander shrugged. "Where do I sign?"

The contract was inked, they all shook hands. The studio boys would be there in a little more than an hour. There wasn't much else to do but sit around and wait for them.

Then the intercom on the conference room table buzzed, and Charlie pushed the button. Maria's voice said, "Mrs. Franklin is here. She says it's urgent."

"Send her up." He looked questioningly at Zander, who didn't seem entirely surprised. I looked at Greg, who shrugged.

The elevator dinged and I looked through the glass wall at Sheila as she stepped off. She didn't look her normal perky self. One could say she looked disheveled, bedraggled almost. Her hair was a mess, her skin all red and blotchy. She looked like she might have been crying, but then I realized it was probably just her allergies acting up.

She entered the conference room, and we all looked expectantly at her. All of us, that is, except for Zander, who looked at his hands, stretched out in front of him on the conference table.

Sheila was having an allergic attack, but she may've been crying, too, after all. She was breathless and just a tiny bit hysterical when she said, "Did you tell them, Jake?"

Zander continued to look at his hands, and for an agonizing split second, I thought this had to have something to do with our little interlude; suddenly I thought that maybe he'd said something to her; or maybe she just suspected something.

But when Zander still didn't speak, Sheila said, "Oh, hi, Marina, how are you?" in her nicest, most pleasant voice. I knew then that, whatever *this* was, it didn't have anything to do with me. Relief sung through my heart.

I opened my mouth to say that I was fine, but nothing came out. I cleared my throat and managed to get it out this time. She smiled at me, then turned to her husband again. "Did you tell them, Jake?" she repeated.

We all looked at him. His head dropped, then he looked up. "Sheila wants to go home."

Greg and I looked at each other, mirrored expressions, identical shocked surprise. Zander continued to look at his hands.

Charlie said, "You can't be serious, Sheila. He just signed a contract." The intercom buzzed again and Charlie savagely pushed the button. "What now?"

Maria's voice said, "Mr. Mariani from the studio just called to say they're running late. Traffic. Said they should be here by 3:30, 3:45 at the latest."

"Great. Thanks."

Sheila said, "You have to fix it, Charlie. I just can't stand it here another minute! The heat, the food! My allergies are killing me! I'm so homesick! It'll only be for a little while. A month . . . Maybe two. Then we'll come back."

Greg looked at me. He broke the stunned silence by saying, "We'll you excuse us?" He rose and nodded at me. I scrambled out of my chair and followed him out to the hall.

We walked over by the elevators. I watched through the glass while Sheila and her brother gesticulated at each other. Zander just sat there looking at his hands.

I looked at Greg. "What the *hell*?"

"I had a hunch this might be coming. She has *not* been having a good time. She said the only fun she's had since we've arrived was when you guys went shopping. She's going to blow it for him."

"Can't she just go back to Canada by herself?"

He smiled bitterly. "Wouldn't that be great? But no. She never goes anywhere without him. For the last twenty years, she has always been there. On the set, at hearings. Conventions. But she never got in the way before. She never tried to pull anything like this."

White hot anger and hatred flashed through my head. My ears started to ring. I said. "Will you excuse me, Greg? I have to get some air."

He said, "Yeah, sure."

I pushed the elevator button and the doors opened immediately. I stepped on the elevator. He smiled that bitter smile at me again. But I didn't smile back. I wasn't seeing him anymore.

I was running on auto-pilot now. All the anxiety and jealousy and hatred that had so dissipated came flooding back, tenfold. That *stupid bitch*, my mind said. *She's trying to take him away. She's going to ruin his career.* The words kept repeating over and over in my head.

I stopped by my office, picked up my purse, walked back out to the elevators. I pushed the button for the lobby, walked out to the parking lot, got in my car, drove home. My anger seethed. I could taste it. That worthless bitch! She was going to take him away, back to fucking Canada.

Yes, indeedy, I was on auto-pilot now. Insane, incensed auto-pilot. No reason, no consequences. Just action. I went into the house, went upstairs, unlocked the door to the attic. I pushed a big box containing an artificial Christmas tree out of the way. Underneath it was a gun case.

The case contained a SIG-Sauer sniper rifle, unlicensed, illegal. My father had received it on the down low from one of his shadier customers, in trade for replacing a blown head gasket on the guy's vintage Corvette. It was one Dad had never let Mom even know he had. But I knew. I'd shot it before. It was a sweet, balanced, lightweight tool, deadly accurate.

I took the gun case downstairs, opened it, and checked the rifle, made sure I had ammo. I grinned without humor, having completely lost my mind. A tool for killing people. One person in particular.

I snapped the case closed, locked up the house. I put the rifle in the trunk of my car, drove back to the office. But I didn't park in the parking lot. Instead, I drove into the parking garage across the street, drove all the way up to the roof. There was always plenty of spots up there. No one wanted to travel all the way down to the street from the roof.

I took the gun case out of the trunk and carried it over to the side of the garage, the side that faced the firm's building, where I would have a clear shot at somebody coming out of the building. Somebody in particular. I took the rifle out of the case. I leaned the case against the guardrail, and then leaned the rifle against the case.

All action, no thought. No future, no consequences. She was trying to take him away. And for no good reason, either. It wasn't because she'd suddenly found out that I loved him. It was just because she was a selfish *bitch*. She was going to take him away, ruin his chance to make it here in the States. I couldn't let her do that.

I called Greg and asked him if Sheila was still there.

"Yeah," he said, sounding surprised. "I'm still standing out here in the hall, looking out the window, like an idiot. I'm not going back in there. There's nothing I can say. Where did you go?"

"I'll see you later," I told him and disconnected. I stood there next to the rifle and waited. No thought, no future.

Then my phone rang again. It was Greg. I hit *Ignore*.

It rang again. He texted: *What are you doing on the roof?*

Shocked, I looked around. He was not there.

He texted again: *I'm looking right at u. Look up. Across. U know what floor I'm on.*

I looked across at the building where I worked, counted up eight floors, two above the roof of the parking garage. I had no trouble at all making him out, standing at the window, waving at me.

He texted: *What's that next to you? Looks almost like a skateboard. A long board.*

My mind came back to me then. The hatred and anger were still there, but diminished, put back somewhere near their proper perspective. I wrote: *I told u. I had 2 get some air. Meet me in the lobby.*

I watched him nod, wave, walk away from the window. When I was sure he was gone, probably already on the elevator, I put the rifle back in its case, and put the case back in the trunk of my car. I rode the grimy elevator down to the first floor of the garage and walked across the street.

Greg was waiting for me in the lobby, talking on his phone. He tilted his head curiously at me, squinted. He said, "Great," into his phone and disconnected. He still squinted at me. "Are you okay?"

I looked blankly at him. "Yeah. I'm okay."

He continued to look curiously at me for another second, and then shrugged it off. "Good news. That was Zander on the phone. Charlie managed to talk her out of it. Promised to get her an appointment with the best allergist in town."

Good, I thought. *For her sake.*

"And here come the suits." Greg nodded out the window. A black limousine had pulled up. Two smartly dressed men stepped out. We watched them as they entered the building, walked past us, waited for the elevator. When the doors opened and they boarded, Greg said, "You look like you could use a drink."

"Don't you have to go up to the meeting?"

He grinned. "Nah. That's what we're paying Charlie the big bucks for. I just book conventions. Send out autographed pictures. I'm the one with my finger on the pulse of the Canadian fan girl when it comes to Jake Franklin, but I don't know anything about dealing with a Hollywood studio.

"Besides, Zander already signed the contract. The rest of this meeting is just a formality; they want to meet him, shake his hand, that kind of stuff. Let's go to *Paul's* for a quick one. We should have just enough time before they're done."

As we walked down the street toward the restaurant, he said, "Thank God for Charlie, though. I think he's the only one who could've talked Sheila out of dragging him back up North. Zander sure dodged a bullet this time."

Or someone did, I thought. I smiled brilliantly at Greg, all trace of my insane berserker rage gone. She would never know just how close she'd come, *how close I'd come* to splattering her brains all over the sidewalk.

Greg and I slammed a quick drink, then Zander called to tell us the meeting was over. The five of us reunited in the lobby and there were many smiles, much backslapping and congratulations. Even Sheila looked a little less blotchy and puffy. I gave her a big hug, saying, "I'm so glad that you decided to stay!"

So I didn't have to kill you, I thought.

She just smiled and nodded, obviously a trifle embarrassed at the little theater of histrionics that she'd staged.

"This calls for a celebration!" Charlie said, and again I cringed at the cliché. "Where should we go?"

"I'm tired of restaurant food," Sheila peeped, not really a whine. She said to Greg, "Didn't you barbeque last night? Can we do that again?"

He nodded and looked at me. "Sounds like a plan," I said.

It was decided that Charlie would take Zander and Sheila to the store for more meat, and Greg would ride back with me. As we rode up the elevator to the roof of the parking garage he asked, "Why did you park all the way over here again?"

"I told you. I had to get some air. A roof is a great place to get some air."

THIRTY-SIX

So, another evening of eating and drinking and loud music and celebration ensued. Things were a little more subdued, however: Charlie and I had to go to work the next day, so Charlie didn't drink anything, and I confined myself to slowing nursing a Grolsch.

I didn't change out of my suit and heels, however, kind of as a celebratory gesture. Charlie probably thought I did it for him, the deluded sod, because he'd gone on and on about how great I looked earlier in the day. But words were not necessary. That look Zander had given me across the office - that was all that was needed for me to stay dressed up.

There was no dancing, either. Greg warned me before I even suggested it, as if I would even suggest it. *As if I would want to watch Zander dance with his wife.* Turns out that Sheila didn't like to dance, felt uncomfortable twirling around in front of other people, Greg said. Why was I not surprised?

Greg made another pitcher of Bloody Caesars. Turned out Caesars were something Sheila *did* like, and it again inspired me to think, *why am I not surprised?*

The music blared, so loud that you couldn't hear yourself think; we'd turned it up so we could hear it in the backyard. But now Greg, Zander and Charlie were in the house, gathered around the grands' old battered dining room table, now loaded with food. The sun was just going down.

Sheila was in the backyard, admiring the garden. I yelled at Greg that I was going to go out and get her. He yelled at me to hold on. He put his cigarette in his mouth, and poured a great generous helping of tomato juice-colored vileness into a glass.

"Here," he shouted. "Take her her drink."

I took it from him and walked into the kitchen, and for no logical reason whatsoever, the idea struck me that I should carry Sheila's drink out to her like a cocktail waitress. So I picked up a little plate from the sink and balanced the glass on it, and walked out the back door and down the three steps. Sheila was standing beside the beehives, bent over a little, her hands on her knees, admiring some little patch of flowers that grew there. She turned her head and smiled at me.

I smiled back and continued my waitress shtick, thrusting the little plate with her drink on it into the air, balanced on my fingers. Then I attempted to negotiate the soft ground between the patio and the beehives, where Sheila stood. I attempted to cross the soft ground in my high heels.

I almost made it. But not quite.

As I walked past the first hive, my heel tangled in a root or a hole or something. On a cheaper pair of shoes, the heel probably would've snapped right off. But not these shoes. The heel stuck fast, and I fell right onto the second beehive, knocking it over on top of Sheila, who went down, splayed out flat on her back.

The lid of the hive flew off and landed by her elbow. The hive itself landed on her abdomen, the frames spilling out across her chest and arms and face. It would've almost been funny if it hadn't been for the bees; the bees roiling out, angry. They crawled on her face, in her hair, on her arms and body, in her mouth.

The bees had all tumbled out of the *top* of the hive. They were all on her. I was on the ground behind the hive, and I didn't get stung once. I was transfixed, down on my hands and knees for what seemed like minutes, watching the bees crawling on Sheila, watching her writhing around on the ground, trying to push the wooden box of the hive off of herself, the sticky, honey-loaded frames. It couldn't have been more than seconds, really, but I wasn't able to move until the bees started stinging her. One, two, ten, fifty, a hundred, a thousand. There could've been tens of thousands of bees in that hive, and now it seemed that they were all buzzing angrily around her head, crawling on her, stinging her.

She started to scream and I finally pushed myself off the ground and tried to run for the door. I fell again, one shoe came off, and I scraped my leg from the knee to the ankle. I looked at the open door to the house as I pushed myself up again. Why weren't they coming to help? Couldn't they hear her screaming?

Finally, I managed to stagger up the stairs and through the kitchen. None of them looked in my direction, for the same reason that they couldn't hear Sheila screaming: the music was too loud.

They stood around the table, laughing, smiling, drinks in hand, a perfect little circle of happiness, unaware that doom was about to fall.

I staggered into the dining room and gasped out, "Zander! Sheila! *The bees!*"

The smile fled from his face and he raced outside, followed by Charlie. Greg caught me before I could fall again. "What happened?" he yelled over the music.

The song ended and in the second of silence that followed, I gasped out, "I tripped. Root or something. Tangled my heel. I fell. Knocked the beehive over on Sheila."

He sat me down quickly in one of the dining room chairs as the driving beat of some other disco song began. I kicked off my other shoe and tried to stand up. I sunk back into the chair, then managed it on the second try, and staggered back out to the back yard.

Zander had thrown the hive off of her, along with the frames. He and Greg were picking her up off the ground and carrying her toward the house, flinching every time they got stung. A little ways away, Charlie was screaming into his phone. He waved his other hand around frantically, trying to keep from getting stung.

They carried Sheila out to Charlie's car, and placed her in the backseat. Zander got in and cradled her head in his lap. Greg got in the front seat. Over the noise of the music that still blared from the house, Charlie yelled, "We're taking her to Community!"

He leapt in the car and sped away. I went back into the house and shut the stereo down. I found a pair of flip flops lying on the bathroom floor, put them on and then jumped in my car and followed them to Community Hospital.

It was all like a movie after that, some hackneyed hospital drama.

I burst through the doors to the emergency room. Greg looked up, strode over and embraced me. "They're back there with her now," he said.

We sat down in the waiting room and held hands. A nurse came out and insisted on looking at the bleeding scrape on my leg. I told her that it was nothing, that my friend's sister-in-law was in the back, that if she wanted to help me, she could go back there and help her. Finally, she left me alone. It was only a scrape after all.

Then the nurse noticed the angry red welts that dotted Greg's hands and arms, his face. She led him to an examining room to remove the stingers. I was left alone in the eerie quiet of the ER waiting room.

After about a half an hour, Greg came back out. "Anything?"

I shook my head. But it wasn't long after that Zander and Charlie came back out. Zander put his arms around his brother's neck and clung to him, crying piteously. Great, wracking sobs. I thanked God that Charlie didn't want to hang onto me and cry. He just stood there silently, the tears rolling down his cheeks and splashing onto the shiny hospital linoleum.

All the epinephrine and albuterol and antihistamines in the world hadn't been enough to save Sheila. She'd just been too allergic, there had just been too many stings. Sheila was gone.

The doctor came out and tried to talk to Zander. But Zander just clung to Greg and cried. After a second of this, Greg passed him off to me, and talked to the doctor. I held him; he cried like it seemed he could never stop. Charlie just stood there and stared at the floor.

After a minute, Greg came back from talking to the doctor. Zander was still crying, but the vehemence of it was subsiding a little bit. Greg said, "Take him home. You got any sedatives, any tranquilizers?" I nodded. It was all too much like a movie. "Give him one. I'll take care of Charlie."

THIRTY-SEVEN

When we got back to my house, I offered Zander a Valium, just like Greg had told me to do. He didn't want it. He lay on the couch, and put his head in my lap. Any bee stings that he'd sustained had already faded. Zander was not at all allergic.

I stroked his hair and cooed to him while he cried. When at last the tears stopped, I took him upstairs and put him in my bed, fully clothed. I covered him with a blanket and he turned over and went immediately to sleep.

I went back downstairs and finally changed out of my suit, the skirt stained and shredded. I wadded it up and stuffed it in the trash. The jacket, too. I stood there in my slip and cleaned up the kitchen, cleared the dining room table, threw away all the uneaten food. I looked out into the backyard. *All that* would just have to wait until tomorrow. I turned out all the lights.

I stood in the shower until the water ran cold, washing off all the blood and dirt and hospital stink that still clung to me. Then I put on some sweats and a t-shirt that were hanging on the back of the bathroom door and went upstairs to check on Zander.

The curtains were open and there was a moon. He was sleeping on his back, and by its light, I could see him clearly. I approached and gazed down at his face. Here was something you didn't find on the internet: any kind of image of the beloved sleeping. This was something only family, only loved ones saw. I longed to touch him, but I didn't want to risk waking him up.

I turned to tiptoe back out of the room again, but the floor creaked, and his eyes fluttered open. "I didn't mean to wake you," I whispered.

"It's okay."

"Can I get you anything?" He shook his head. I said, "Goodnight, then, Zander."

I again turned toward the door, and he said, "Don't go." I looked back. "Come here. Lie down by me for a minute."

I slowly climbed into the bed next to him and he enfolded me in his arms. I laid my head on his chest. I said, "I'm so sorry, Zander." And I *was* sorry, sorry for his pain, his tears, his loss.

"It was an accident. It wasn't your fault."

I didn't think it was my fault. In fact, I thought it was only my good fortune. A turned heel, a broken glass, a turned over beehive, and here I was lying in bed next to him. But it was all right if he thought that I blamed myself. I probably should've blamed myself, but I didn't. It was an accident, after all. Why had her dumb allergic ass been standing so close to the fucking beehives anyway, for Christ's sake?

We lay there in silence for some time, and I thought that he'd fallen asleep again. But when I looked up at him, his eyes were open. He looked at me solemnly with those deep blue eyes, then slowly leaned forward and kissed me. It wassn't a passionate kiss - more one born out of a desire for a little human contact in grief.

But his kiss didn't remain that way for long. Before I knew it, he was kissing me fervently, hungrily, pulling my hair and twisting my head to meet his. Before I knew it, we were taking off our clothes. Before I knew it, he rolled me over on top of him and there I was, impaled upon Jackson Alexander Franklin.

Words do not exist to describe the perfect bliss, the utter, mindless release. It was all of the orgasms of a thousand lifetimes, detonating simultaneously. It was . . . *fruition*. And then it only got better after that.

We made love; over and over again, until, tangled in the sheets, tangled in each other, we passed out. If it had been a movie, Etta James would've been singing in the background. *And here we are in heaven/For you are mine at last.*

THIRTY-EIGHT

I was suddenly awake, but I didn't open my eyes, didn't move. I couldn't remember where I was. I thought back, remembered a dream I'd been having about Zander. I dreamed that we'd been making love, savagely, slowly, sweetly, *continuously* . . . And then he moved against me in his sleep, and I opened my eyes. I still believed myself to be dreaming for another second, and then it all came back. I caressed his cheek, his bare shoulder.

Then it hit me that I was ravenously hungry, that I hadn't eaten anything for what seemed like days. I slid out of bed slowly, carefully, so as not to wake him. I paused to look at him, so beautiful in sleep. I couldn't locate my sweats, and figuring that they had to be lost in the sheets somewhere, I snatched a robe off of a chair, tiptoed out and quietly pulled the door closed.

I walked downstairs and almost had the living daylights scared out of me when I found Greg sitting in my living room, smoking one of his Canadian menthols. He knew where the key was, under the green flowerpot, so he'd just gone ahead and let himself in.

He sighed. "We need to talk, Marina." He spun a compact disk on the coffee table, like a top. I watched it dance across the glass, glittering, before finally clattering to a stop. I couldn't be sure, but I thought it might be the disk with all the pictures of Zander on it, because it was unlabeled.

I looked at him. He said, "Pardon my snooping around in your desk, looking at your computer. But I had to do something while I was waiting for you two to stop thrashing around up there."

He snuffed his cigarette out, sighed again. "Have you not gone by the username *PhiliMarina665* on the internet?" He pulled a wrinkled scrap of paper out of his pocket. "Did you not once send an email to someone who calls herself

CanadaBees, that read, and I quote, 'While I am new to the amazing universe of Jackson Alexander Franklin, I would not have found it such a splendid place indeed had it not been for your site?'"

I stared at him in disbelief. He stared right back at me. At last I mumbled, "She never answered that email."

"Oh, but she posted it," he said. He looked at the paper again. "Just last week."

"I haven't been on her site for a long time."

I sat down in a chair that had an unimpeded view of the steps that led upstairs. I was confident that Zander wouldn't be able to accidently wander into *this* conversation: the door was closed, the floor squeaked and I would hear him if he got up. But I wanted to be doubly sure, wanted to know that I could tell Greg to *shut the fuck up* if I sensed that Zander was within earshot.

Greg was saying, "One crazy bitch is *CanadaBees*, let me tell you. I met her at a convention last year. She's like twenty years old, did you know that? He's almost old enough to be her father, for Christ's sake."

I'd surmised as much from a certain juvenile cast to her commentary, clever as it was. I remained silent.

"But you! You take the fucking crazy prize. I suspected that you were one of them all along. I didn't even really have to do a search for your username, the one that you were too dumb to change even slightly from the same email that you use to this day." He gestured at the laptop sitting on the desk, still hooked up to the stereo. "You fan girls, you can't really disguise it, try as you might. It shows in the way you look at him, a certain little hesitation in replying when he speaks to you."

He crumpled the piece of paper up and threw it on the coffee table. I leaned forward immediately and snatched it up, along with the CD, which I quickly, viciously snapped in half.

"I know how it is with you people, laying in your little beds at night, thinking about him, *fantasizing* about him, imagining all the filthy little things that you would do to him, all the filthy little things you want him to do to you." He grinned at me. "Yeah, I always thought that *CanadaBees* was the number one nutjob, but you - you leave her completely in the dust.

"You orchestrated this whole thing," he said in wonderment. "First, it must've been Charlie. It had to have started with him. How did you snare Charlie?"

It started with Zander, I thought.

I sighed. No sense holding back now. "I saw *The Beekeeper* for the first time on *Netflix* one weekend. I apparently don't need to tell you that I was immediately hooked." Now Greg remained silent. "It's Canadian. Charlie's Canadian. I went into the office on Monday morning and asked him if he'd ever heard of Jake Franklin. That's when he dropped the bombshell on me: that he was, in fact, *Jake Franklin's brother-in-law*, that the object of my filthy little fantasies would be coming to our very office in a few months to negotiate a movie deal. So, actually, it all started out as one big, colossal, unbelievable fucking coincidence."

"And making Charlie fall in love with you? That was easy."

"Charlie was already in love with me," I replied flatly. "Had been so for years. I'd just never acknowledged it before."

"And then there were the bees. You sucked him in with all your convenient knowledge about the fucking bees. I knew the goddamn bees would be his downfall someday."

They certainly were Sheila's downfall, I thought, and suppressed an entirely not apropos smirk.

As if reading my mind, Greg said, "Then you turn around and *kill his wife*."

"Lower your voice," I growled. "I did *not* kill his wife. *It was an accident.*"

"Yeah, and this. This was almost an accident, too."

He took his phone from his pocket and pushed a button, held it up so I could see it. It was a picture of me, taken from the eighth floor of my own office building. There I was in that exquisite black suit, standing next to something that was clearly, definitely *not* a longboard. The case might've looked a little like one, but there was no mistaking what was leaning against it.

"The camera on that phone has awesome range," I marveled.

"What the fuck were you thinking?"

I shrugged, looked at the floor. "I went a little crazy. She was going to take him away." Greg shook his head in amazement. I looked up at him. "So what do you intend to do about all this?"

"I have a little story to tell you, a little story of several parts, and I predict that you are not going to *fucking* believe it. Remember, I promised you one time that I would tell you the story about how Zander and Sheila originally hooked up?"

I nodded. Poor, dead Sheila. I felt nothing at all for her except gratitude that she was gone.

"You are familiar with Meatloaf's *Paradise by the Dashboard Light*?"

I looked at him in amazement. "It was like that? They seemed so happy." I paused and couldn't help a little smile. "Then the bees did him a favor. Set him free."

"Zander never broke his promise or forgot his vow. And while I'm sure that he loved her, twenty years is a long time. And she could be a drag. God only knows what he's done right now," he paraphrased Meatloaf absently.

"So, what now?" I asked.

"Ah, wait awhile, my friend." Greg held up his finger. "There is quite a bit more to this story. There is quite a little something that you don't know about me. *That you don't know about Zander.* That nobody knows.

"Allow me to set the scene for you, and then you can just let that phenomenal imagination of yours run fucking wild. I apologize in advance if you get turned on, but then you can always just go back upstairs and take it out on him.

"It was summertime. Don't you find sex is so much better in the summertime? The heat, the sweat?"

"Just tell the story."

"Okay. He was out, on the boulevard somewhere, where he was not supposed to be. It was way past curfew and he didn't want to let Mom know he hadn't come in yet, didn't want Mom to maybe figure out what he'd been up to. So he climbed up the side of the house and came into our room through the open window.

"Ah, that room we shared! It was like something out of the best porn. Two narrow beds, teenaged boys' beds, separated by a night stand. We used to lay there, in the dark, and talk about our dreams. Well, he would talk about *his* dreams.

"My dreams, you see, were all about *him*. I'd been in love with Zander from the moment I saw him standing there at our parents' wedding in his rented tux. Why else would I have stayed on with them, in that one horse town? So I didn't talk much. Just listened to the sound of his voice in the heat, in the cold of winter." I looked at him then, nonplussed. He smirked. "I told you that you wouldn't fucking believe it.

"Anyway, he climbed in the window, and I was sitting on my bed, waiting for him. I could tell by the look on his face that it had happened. He'd talked about her before, told me how pretty she was. Told me that he liked her. Told me that he was going out to see her that night.

"You have to picture him, my friend. He was seventeen, sweaty, disheveled, nervous. Those incredible blue eyes glowed by the light of the one small lamp. Fresh from fucking that stupid farm girl. He just looked at me, his expression unreadable, but like he wanted to say something to me, explain, apologize. I stood and approached him. He stood stock still, waiting.

"I kissed him right on the mouth, that heavenly, perfect mouth. He shoved me across the room, exactly the reaction I had been expecting, the reaction of any red-blooded, heterosexual Canadian boy, fresh from deflowering his little backward girlfriend.

"But he didn't move, didn't speak. He just stood there, panting a little bit now. The lamp had fallen off the night stand when he pushed me. It was laying sideways on the floor, and he cast a black shadow on the wall, all his angelic features in sharp relief. I know you can picture it, Marina. He was wearing some kind of wife beater, and the muscles of his arms and neck stood out like he was made of marble. That hell black hair, all messed up, the blue eyes blazing, the angelic lips parted, his breath coming in short gasps. But he didn't move.

"Can you picture it, Marina? The object of all your deepest desires, standing there looking at me, only seventeen?"

"You know that I can, Greg." I found that I was panting a little myself. "Tell your story."

"I picked myself up off the floor, and approached him again. He didn't move. This time, I took the beloved face in both hands, ran my hands through those black curls, pulled his head to me and kissed him again. He resisted for a split second, and then all at once he was kissing me back.

"We fell back on his little boy's bed, and it collapsed under our weight. We paused, listening to see if Mom and Dad had heard the crash, but not a sound came from downstairs.

"Then he looked at me and tangled his hands in *my* hair and pulled my face to him, all pretense gone now. He kissed me just like I'd always dreamed he would, just like *you've* always dreamed he would."

Like he just did, I thought.

"'Now I'm gonna give you what you really want,' I told him, and he just looked at me, those baby blues filled with longing. And I proceeded. I could taste that bitch on him, but I didn't care, because I knew that he wasn't thinking about her. He was only thinking about me, *his brother*, the one he'd wanted all along. To this day, he gets the same look in his eyes. And I can always picture him, just as he was that first time, hot and sweaty, wanting me utterly, only seventeen."

This was really all too much, too much entirely, and I got up, shook one of his *Dunhills* out of its strange, long pack, and lit it with the lighter that had been lying beside it on the coffee table.

I sat back down and Greg continued. "In the morning, he confessed what he'd done, that he'd liked it well enough, that she'd made him promise to marry her first, that manipulative bitch.

"'But it was nothing like this,' he told me, anguish in the angelic eyes, those beautiful, beautiful eyes. Those eyes that should never have to bear such an expression.

"'It's okay,'" I told him, and kissed his eyebrows. 'It'll all work out.'

"'But I can't marry her now!' he cried. 'You ... this... this is what I want!'

Oh, yeah, this is entirely too much, I thought, and puffed reflexively on my cigarette. Greg gestured to me, and I handed it to him, and he took a long drag.

"God, I love menthols," he said.

"Finish your fucking story!" I growled.

He looked at me in surprise. "Well, you know the rest. It's the fairytale romance of the century in Canada, known by heart by every fan girl. He married his childhood sweetheart in a quaint country church, the following year. He was only eighteen; she was not quite seventeen. His brother was his best man. There was no money for a honeymoon, but he is - *was* - always taking her on second honeymoons, much to the sighs of the fan girls."

I never sighed over that shit, I thought.

"Instead of a honeymoon, the three of us pooled our money, and headed out to the big city, to make him famous. *That was my idea.* He did a little modeling - that crazy bitch *CanadaBees* even dug up some of those old ads from somewhere."

I had seen them. Some of them were on the disk that I'd just snapped in half.

I said, "And Sheila never knew about the two of you? About your . . . Your *relationship?* She never guessed?"

"Of course not. Did you guess?"

I shook my head. Not in a million years. Despite what Greg had just told me, it seemed to me, from the exuberance and skill of his lovemaking, that Zander liked women well enough. It seemed that he liked *me* well enough.

Greg continued, "He did some theater, then got his break with the bee show. He got the reputation as a goody-two shoes, from playing that character; good and pure is our Zander, tied to the land, desperately and forever in love with his farm-girl wife. That's what everybody thinks, anyway. Do I need to go on? You know the story as well as anybody."

"Now his farm girl wife is dead."

"Oh, and what a tragedy that is, is it not? There's going to have to be some damage control on this one, though. Thank God it happened in the States. If it had happened in Canada, the banner headline in the *Toronto Star* would scream: *The Beekeeper's Wife Stung to Death!* We'll just have to put it out that it was some kind of an allergic reaction, but try to somehow leave the bees out of it."

"So what happens now?"

"Well, I can tell you what *he'll* want to do. First he'll say, 'Fuck this movie, the contract be damned. Let 'em sue me.' And they *will* sue him. Hollywood doesn't care if your wife dies. A contract is a contract. No codicils about fatal allergic reactions.

"Then after they sue him, he'll want to take all of the money that he has left and buy a little island in the Territories, and live there in bliss, with a little garden and a few beehives." He paused and grinned his demonic grin at me. "*With me.* He's talked about it before."

I stared at him, open-mouthed, thinking that this was *just* how things always worked out for me. Always was I eventually denied. So close, and yet inevitably, so impossibly far.

Then Greg said, "But we can't let him do that, now can we, my friend?"

I just looked at him.

"We can't let him throw away his career. This movie might just be his break out in the States. I think it's a piece of shit, but he might be able to carry it off. I know all the fan girls will stand in line in the snow to see it in Canada. Their pity and their love will damn near overwhelm them, after they hear about how he carried on gamely and finished it, even after his wife died.

"But if he quits - *retires*, if you will - and we go off together, unkind tongues will wag. Someone might bring up the fact that we're not actually brothers by blood. Someone will note my lack of a girlfriend all my life. We'll be discovered in our sin.

"We can't have the world find out that Canada's favorite son is gay, now can we? Or even bisexual. There's not *that* much money left, even before the studio sues him. He'd never work again."

"So what are you saying, Greg?" I thought that predicting that he would never work again might be a little dramatic.

"I like you, Marina. More importantly for all of us, *he* likes you. He has dipped his wick, shall we say, into the heterosexual pool again, with you. Having a woman every twenty years or so, it's good for a person. I try to do it myself, at least once every twenty years." He showed all his teeth. "And he couldn't have picked one better looking than you, I must say. I would've picked you myself, maybe, if there hadn't been all those Charlie complications. But I would've broken your heart eventually." Still, he grinned at me.

Greg couldn't even imagine how much that *never* would've happened. Not with Zander around. He only dreamt that he knew the depth of my devotion, if he believed I would've done anything with him, once I actually met Zander. Poor Charlie had been left behind almost from the second that they'd stepped onto American soil.

And I would've become a nun before I would've ever let anyone touch me again, once Zander started smiling at me, dancing with me. Once I kissed Zander, there would be no other. Ever.

"Yeah," Greg was saying, "you've wormed your way completely into his heart, with your devious research, your planning, your manipulation. Your perfect little house and garden. *Your fucking bees.* Your adoration."

When I looked surprised, he said, "Yeah, he sees it too. How could he miss it? But you've kept the crazy hidden well enough that he just thinks it's a mutual thing. He thinks that it's something unexpected, something that's just *bloomed* since the two of you met. Not something that you planned from the start."

I couldn't have dreamed that all my planning would go so well, *however,* I thought, and that smirk reappeared on my face.

Greg said, "What I want to know is, how can you stand that terrible beer?"

I shrugged. "Allowances must be made."

"Indeed. Here is my plan, take it or leave it. I propose that after a suitable period of mourning for the farm girl, you and our beloved one get married." He paused to let that one sink it.

"He finishes the movie, becomes a big American movie star, and after awhile the *three of us* retire to that island in the Territories. I'm willing to share him with you, if you're willing to share him with me.

"Hell, I put up with Sheila for twenty years, and you're already *so much* more fun than she *ever* was. A fucking sniper rifle? I can't wait to see what comes next.

"And I'm not such a bad guy, once you get to know me. We can each behold those perfect eyes until we're all old and gray. What do you say?"

I could not speak. When I didn't answer him immediately, Greg took my hesitation for something that it wasn't. He seemed to think that I might be considering turning down his offer. *As if.*

He said, "Or, you could try to expose us, try to destroy him. And then, or course, I'd have to expose *you* for what you really are, what you've really been all along, nothing but a quite unhinged fan girl.

"Of course, the damage to his career would probably already be done. You intimate that someone's gay once, and it sticks in people's minds. He'd have no other choice but to retire with me to that island after all. Maybe he'd even be relieved to have it all out it the open. But his image, his career would be ruined.

"And then there would be all those questions about how you insinuated yourself into our lives, how it was *you* who accidentally knocked that box of death over onto his wife. Maybe I'd just have to anonymously release this picture of you with that fine automatic weapon."

Still I could not speak.

"But mostly, most importantly of all, you would hurt him, Marina. You would hurt him to the bone. The man that you've wanted utterly since you first saw him on your tiny little TV, since you first downloaded his picture on your woeful little virus-laden computer, the man you love with every cell in your body. You would hurt him, and you'd never see him again.

"Or the two of you could just go your separate ways, sans any revelations about sexual orientation. After he finishes this movie, he could go back to Canada and soldier on. You could go back to living your little life. Maybe patch things up completely with Charlie. Settle down, have some kids." Greg paused again to let *that* suicidal-thought inducing scenario sink in. Then he said, "I think Zander has fallen in love with you, Marina, as much as he can love a woman. As much as he can love anyone that's not me." He grinned. "But I'll see to it that he gets over it. Maybe I'll find some other substitute to marry him. Maybe I'll make some other fan girl's dream come true. Paging *CanadaBees!* Jesus, we can't have him single, the fan girls will camp out, and I'll never have a moment's peace. I'll send you a postcard sometimes. An invitation to the wedding."

"I thought you people were supposed to be proud of your . . . Your *preferences*. I thought you didn't go in for hiding it."

He smiled at me with his killer shark's grin. "I am proud of my preference, at least as proud of it as you are of yours, seeing as it's the same preference. And I am a whole lot more secure in my position than you are. But my preference, his preference . . . *Your preference*, for that matter, and your insane devotion to it - that's all nobody's business but ours.

"We have to live in the world we live in, Marina. Zander is an actor. In Canada, he's a fucking *celebrity*. And as such, he has a certain image that must be maintained. And that image is of a heterosexual. If nothing else, it's how he earns his money.

"I'm not ashamed of us. I love him. But still, it's all nobody else's business. That's why they call them *closed doors*. What goes on behind them is *private*. Not for mass consumption. Not because I'm ashamed of it, but because it's *mine* and *his*. And yours, if you want it to be. And oh, my God, if he came out, then I'd have eight million crazy fan *boys* to deal with, too. No thanks."

He paused, then grinned slyly at me. "He already has a small but quite *devoted* following on that score as it is. Do you know what *slashfiction* is, Marina?"

"I do not."

"It's a subgenre of fan fiction, written by homosexuals about heterosexual characters. From TV, movies, video games. You know, Kirk on Spock, that kind of thing. There's quite a collection out there on the internet concerning *The Beekeeper* and the guy that played the other scientist. It's not only women who have dirty little fantasies about him, you see."

What a wicked world we live in, I thought. I wondered if *CanadaBees* knew about this.

"Zander absolutely *loves* it," Greg said. "I read them aloud to him sometimes. They make him giggle *hysterically.* Sometimes we even -"

"I'll do it," I said, all hesitation gone.

There had never really been any hesitation, anyway. It had just taken me a moment to *assimilate* everything. Would I be willing to *marry* Jackson Alexander Franklin? Me? *Hot damn*, how could Greg think that I would hesitate for even one moment? One does not hesitate to acquiesce to their most impossible dreams.

And I actually did like Greg, even if he *had* had it in for me all along, even if I'd never fooled him for even a split second.

That devil's grin again. He said, "I knew that you would. You will save us all from ourselves, and your reward will be . . . Well, you know what your reward will be. What more can any unhinged fan girl ask for?"

And the rest, as they say, is history. I've even gotten used to the winters. And sometimes, when it's really cold outside, the three of us, well, sometimes we . . . Well, you can just use your imagination.

And the water is *awesome*.

****

Also by LM Foster

A Passing Resemblance
Contrariwise – A Tale of Twins
Corvino
Crypsis
Duck Feet
Peter's Sisters

Two Green Keys
Two Green Keys
Adapted for the Screen

One Wilde Ride Trilogy:
Book One: It Might Have Been
Book Two: An Exceptional Boy
Book Three: What Should Never Be

Stars and Guitars:
Talk To a Movie Star
Where The Guitars Play

Tom and Wiley:
This Carnival of Strange
Wiley Royce
Generally Recognized as Safe
Wiley Royce Versus The Martians

www.ingramcontent.com/pod-product-compliance
Lightning Source LLC
Chambersburg PA
CBHW070931130626

46555CB00001B/386